A House Near Luccoli

D.M. Denton

A House Near Luccoli

The events portrayed herein are the author's fictionalized account of a period of time in the life of Alessandro Stradella. Certain historical figures are real; other characters are purely the products of the author's imagination. This work in no way purports to be other than fiction.

ISBN: 978-0-9857789-7-2

Library of Congress Control Number: 2012946909

Cover Art by D.M. Denton

Published in 2012 by All Things That Matter Press

For my mom, June,
and
grandmother, Marion

Acknowledgments

My long hesitant journey to being published is indebted to the loving and honest support and encouragement of my mother, June, who even in her eighties treasures my childhood scribbling with an enthusiasm that still embarrasses me but also reassures me that writing is my true calling. She read this novel more than once, long before anyone else even knew of its existence, and, as the one I share my everyday life with, put up with my disappearances into the hours and months and years between its conception and completion, as well as my fluctuating moods over its progress and possibilities. She is a beautiful, intelligent, and talented woman, a wonderful artist in her own right, who has accomplished a life of integrity, curiosity and compassion, and has always been my greatest inspiration.

In terms of research into the life, character, and music of Alessandro Stradella, I owe much to what is now considered to be the definitive work about him, Carolyn Gianturco's *Alessandro Stradella, His Life and Music* (1994, Oxford University Press), not only for its pages of biography and detailed discussion of his music, but also its inclusion of his extant letters and dedications, examples of his handwritten musical notation and autograph, along with other plates that helped me visualize the people and places that affected him. I am also grateful for the excellent musicians who recorded his music so that I might hear the heart and soul and especially spirit of the man: Estevan Velardi of the Alessandro Stradella Consort and *Camerata Ligure*; Maurizio Fornero of *I Musica di Santa Pelagio*; Marc Minkowski of *Les Musicians du Louvre*; and Michael Schneider of *La Stagione Frankfurt*.

As far as my knowledge of Genoa in the 1680's, I must mention a wonderful out-of-print book I was fortunate to come upon: *Genoa, History and Art in an Old Seaport* by Edmund Howard (first published 1971 by Sagep S.p.A – Genoa). It was invaluable to my research into the city's churches, palaces, plazas, harbor, and other landmarks; but also to my understanding of its layout, culture, history, and overall sense of itself.

I feel strongly that I would not be writing this acknowledgement if it wasn't for the generosity of the gifted novelist, playwright and essayist Marina Julia Neary, who out of the blue very kindly offered to introduce me to her publishers at All Things That Matter Press. From there the blessings increased as I became a part of the ATTMP family, warmly welcomed by its owners, Deb and Phil Harris, and its talented authors. As my editor, I can't thank Deb Harris enough for her patience with correcting my punctuation and misplaced modifiers, noting my propensity to over-poetizing, and in the end helping me to see the novel with new eyes to make it the best it could be. I am forever grateful to her and Phil for this chance to finally see *A House Near Luccoli* published.

One of the most beautiful distinctions of the sun is to disburse the mine of its golden splendors not only over the nearest countries but also to the most remote lands.

~*Alessandro Stradella*
from his dedication of
La forza dell'amor paterno, Genoa 1678

PART ONE

The Arrival
April 1681

CHAPTER ONE

She didn't fuss with her hair or use the vain clutter of the dressing table except to waste time rearranging it. Eventually she turned to what was behind her. Laid over a small unmade bed and the chair beside it were two fancy gowns, creased and dated, suiting a younger shape and needing somewhere to go. She was sure she wouldn't wear them again.

"Donatella? Are you in your room?"

The lace might be salvaged, for she couldn't be without lace, at least around her neck and, at most, edging her sleeves as well. Otherwise she dressed serviceably, invisibly, in gray or dark blue.

She no longer thought of being bolder or more submissive or, in a city on a bay-becoming-the-sea, swept away at last.

It was as if someone else recalled a ship, who sailed on it, and walking down a shady alley with a stranger. There was always the temptation of mixing imagination with reality, especially as the past was otherwise inalterable. Her reflection was plain in the mirror, her hair quickly pinned, her face flushed.

"Donatella, I need you!"

She moved to a corner table, begging light from a narrow window, cleaning brushes and closing colors yet to finish curled pictures of spring or begin the next season before it did. She had painted in brighter places, dreamed in them, too, and didn't care who saw her as a dreamer, until she committed herself to being withdrawn and forgotten like a lunatic huddled in a corner, hardly knowing the difference between a smile and a frown.

"You might answer me!"

She took the green dress off the bed and pretended to wear it for a small stroll around the room. Then she walked into the hall as if out into the city; her city, at least, as it was also born of land and sea, formed by highs and lows, ruled by outer constraint and inner abandon, safe and sorry in disguise. Of course *Genova* had a conceit she couldn't have, knowing its purpose and hiding or flaunting its features of beauty. Once she saw all its wonders and woes from the esplanade of *Castelletto*, the mountains closer and the *Lanterna* further away. Perhaps she made out her house; if not its signature portal of Saint George and the Dragon, then a signifying shine on its roof's slant. It was a prestigious place to live depending on how she looked at it, whether connected up to a parade of palaces, across divides or down crooked stairways to the port.

She was patron and prisoner of a gated entrance and more rooms than the closeness of the surrounding dwellings allowed, aspiring staircases growing them similarly into multiple stories. She could have done without so much unused furniture, mirrors, and silver to be cleaned but was greedily accustomed to a tenanted wealth of paintings, tapestries, frescos, and stained glass not created for outside views.

"There you are. What are you doing?"

Donatella had barely reached the doorway of her bedroom, throwing the dress in, not caring where it landed.

"Oh, it's so sudden."

Her aunt gave her a key and feather duster for gentler work than Nubesta carrying broom and bucket, hastening an end to the long vacancy of the third floor apartment, a little unnerving to step into its past. It offered another chore for the young maid complaining about wiping tall windows while Donatella removed furniture covers and thought of her mother sitting there, writing more letters than she ever received.

The girl opened a window and the room to the street below, a rag-waving hand jumping out. "Up here! Up here!"

Donatella felt a shiver that shouldn't have surprised her, the bumping and cursing of the movers fading into music and poetry from *La forza dell'amor paterno* as performed at the *Teatro Falcone* on Christmas Monday 1678. She had worn the green dress, agreeing to excessive curls and anticipation, Nonna encouraging her to fan away smoke from the chandeliers and smile although her shoes pinched. After the first act sonnets fell from garlanded boxes for those lucky enough to catch them; as much enthusiasm when the opera was finished. That was Donatella's last trembling in applause and first glimpse of its beneficiary too remarkable for humility as he accepted a gold tray of the taffeta wrapped accolades. He was as well presented in a long shimmering coat with flared skirt, accented with a looped and knotted cravat, an undressed wealth of hair changing the angles of his face as he bowed and then again. Obviously this was the legend of subterfuge, here and there, elegant and rakish, kissing the hand of *Centoventi,* goddess of the stage. He was clever and foolish not to worry she took exception at his as intimate approval of the contralto said to be the daughter of a cook, nothing but wisdom and faithfulness in his deepest bow and sincerest smile towards Genoa's Prince and Princess.

Even overlooked in the audience, Donatella felt he was a suitor offering the art of himself. So at least in the theater she could be chosen.

Nothing more intimate was expected, and shouldn't be. Not even when their landlord, one of the Falcone's managers, announced that *Signor Stradella would be moving into their quiet world.*

And unquiet hearts, resentment sounding in Signor Garibaldi's teasing.

Like offering the pigeons to the cat! Aunt Despina couldn't resist.

It was assumed Signor Stradella would use the apartment for composing as well as sleep and light refreshments. Otherwise he would be out for tutoring and rehearsals during the day and church performances on Sundays, his evenings planned and unplanned with meals and diversions in more and less respectable settings.

Two large but struggling men maneuvered in a long walnut trunk with brass filigree corners and latch. They stood looking down the embossed hall to its sun-splashed end.

"Should we leave it here?" one of them asked.

"Why not?" Nubesta decided. "He'll put it where he wants."

"No." Donatella, not for the first time, had to correct her. "In the bedroom."

The men grumbled, did as they were told, then left, returning with musical instruments, a pair of trestles, square board, small stool, and a plainer case rattling with poorly packed contents. The apartment was already furnished, not with the Garibaldi finest, but bees-wax polishing gave console tables, armoire, credenza, and bed posts a higher shine. By the time citywide bells announced the vespers hour, Nubesta was done and resting on a frayed settee without any guilt for Donatella reaching over her to wipe the beveled mirror above.

The movers were less irritated as they brought in one crate dropping heavy and another floating to the floor, talking about where they would go drinking. Nubesta followed them out to be sure they were gone.

"Look." Donatella untied a note from around the handle of the fancier trunk.

"You know I can't read."

"To the most honorable ladies of this household, please make my bed with the hemp sheets, pillowcase and woolen blanket within. A.S."

"Not such a gentleman," Nubesta hoped.

The trunk's carved exterior was scarred and the latch almost fell off when Donatella popped it to fold back the top like a book she shouldn't read and hadn't any reason to beyond the first page, the noted bedding on top. She relied on Nubesta's willingness to go through Signor Stradella's things that were neatly layered and smelled of parchment and resin; no surprise that he owned the finest neckties, cuffs, shirts, jackets, breaches, dressing gown, ribbons, kerchiefs, gloves, stockings, belts, and buckles, and silver instrument strings unwrapped from a silk-velvet cloth.

Nubesta dug a little deeper, discovering two rosaries with gold medals, and a religiously embroidered runner with pointed ends and silk tassels.

"What is it?"

Donatella stretched it out, wondering, too. "A scapular, devoted to St. Dominic."

"Why would he have it?"

"Let's see to the bed."

It seemed a shame to strip already made wealth for grey hemp and brown wool, squeezing a plump pillow like the best sausage meat into a thin and tasteless casement. They pulled the sheets tight, laid out the yarn-hemmed blanket, finishing with a swollen brocade cover-up, the room ready or not for its distinguished if disreputable new occupant. It was the second adjective Nubesta seemed to know the most about, as servants often did, talk amongst themselves both informed and ignorant.

"Another note." The girl tugged at it.

Donatella was already fond of the forwardly fluid and looped handwriting. "Most honorable ladies, I imagine you hesitate. Please feel free to unpack and arrange my effects, like a puzzle, and see if you can know how I would like them. A.S."

"For a prize?" Nubesta squirmed, waiting for Donatella's next move.

"I don't think we should."

"You went through his clothes. What are a few knickknacks after that?"

"Take the cleaning things and tell my aunt we're done."

Nubesta obeyed sluggishly, the late afternoon warming the room's new belongings, the key Donatella tied around her arm under her sleeve too prominent to forget there.

***

She entered the dark room to soft meowing, both cats jumping down from her grandmother's bed.

Nonna stirred a little. "You could copy for him."

"I'm sure he has a copyist. I'm sure he has all he needs."

"He might think so." Nonna pulled her granddaughter's face so close to hers against the pillow Donatella almost laid down. "You shouldn't."

Donatella kissed her grandmother's dry cheek, combing her still thick gray hair, regretting more than that she wasn't a chaperone for the theater any longer. Nonna's hands had lost touch with the virginal, her trained voice weakened to whispers, her appetite merely for bread and broth.

"What's this?" A misshapen hand caught the bulge in Donatella's lower sleeve.

"Oh. The key to ... the ... linen closet."

"Well," Nonna's voice strengthened, "you might keep it, as you never take what isn't yours."

In the middle of the night Donatella rose to a dare and the third floor, bare steps as uncertain as candlelight on an unknown artist's commission of cherubs and festooned fruits and flowers in muted greens, grays, and sienna. The floor of the apartment didn't keep her entry quiet but it seemed only her carefulness was disturbed. The trestle table was set up in the salon, too close to the fireplace with its escalloped oak mantle and triangular copper hood illustrating Vulcan and Venus. Windows on both sides were almost hidden by red curtains with gold scrolling around the Garibaldi coat of arms, the moon somehow casting light on the secrecy of her endeavor. She unpacked Signor Stradella's clothes, carrying the pieces one at a time or in piles to the bedroom and shelves of the wardrobe that threatened to be too small. *He has more of what's necessary and unnecessary than a woman, a much indulged woman*. She opened another trunk holding the rewards of beautiful music, smiles and connivances, too, doubtful he carried the family heirlooms while by invitation or escape running around and hiding. Whatever explained the collection, he was aristocratic in everything but bedding and especially fortunate in moveable assets, even indifferent about some of them with silver candlesticks and snuffers, trays, bowls, spoons, toothpicks, and boxes as tarnished as his reputation.

Silver wasn't unusual in a city where even the lowest had the chore of it in their homes, while gold wasn't to be seen in any ordinary way, and she supposed he took pride in what he had of it, from buttons and medals to a locked tobacco caddy studded with diamonds.

She sensed some fraud, too, and quickly deposited a reliquary with the scapular in the chest at the foot of the bed. Otherwise she arranged with an eye for practical and creative importance, or just not knowing where else to put things without cluttering incidental surfaces and the narrow mantle. A candelabrum belonged on the trestle table as did a bookstand and bundle of folders with ribbons untied for a chance of revelation, placed next to a decorated writing slope for composing more than little notes to honorable ladies.

Three lutes huddled against the emptiness of a corner, stepsisters born separately of rosewood, maple, and ebony, sharing an inheritance of long necks, heads back, full bodies with rosettes like intricately set jewels on their breasts. Theirs was harmonious rivalry, recalling a master's touch and understanding. On the settee a leather case contained a violin resembling a dead man on the red velvet of his coffin, not mourned but celebrated by nymphs dancing through vines on the frieze high around the room.

As nearby *Santa Maria Maddalena* sounded for Lauds, the gold and diamonded box urgently invited investigation. She guessed where the key might be, pressing a button under the ink bottle section of the slope. A sudden drawer offered it, tiny, burnished, a promise of something special, not in that container but the one worth hundreds of *scudi* which instead of tobacco held more diamonds or a love note or pressed flower or curl of hair or ...

An accolade. She recognized the taffeta tied scroll at once, recalling applause that lingered, hearts melting for the music and man and impossibilities he left behind.

"You're in trouble." Nubesta startled Donatella, who could only hope she wasn't seen locking the rolled sonnet away again, placing its treasured box on the lower shelf of the nightstand. "She's looking for the key."

"Here. No." Donatella put a hand behind her back. "Where?"

Nubesta pulled it out of the door more for power than assistance.

"Give it to me."

Donatella waited for Nubesta to leave before returning one key to its almost private place, exiting the apartment herself as the other met Despina's outstretched hand. Her aunt might have wanted an explanation but didn't get one, Donatella escaping to her room to dress hurriedly, stuffing her hair under a cap, then on her way downstairs in time to welcome a man she had never met except as he inspired sonnets and forgetfulness.

CHAPTER TWO

The door opened. A harpsichord entered, hesitant, fragile, blushing and elegant with carved cheeks, perfect curves, and small feet. It was permanently adorned with sprays of roses and fern, lifted over the threshold by a lover who knew how to handle his passion.

He wasn't daunted by the heights to which it must yet be taken. "*Bene*, my *spirito* has ascended her to heaven."

"Now, my muscle, too." A man of lesser age and quality took hold of the instrument's narrowing end, swinging it around and walking backwards, resenting his position.

Despina saw Donatella on the stairs. "Out of the way."

"Ah." The new lodger widened his eyes, conducting the scene into civility. "Golone, let the maid pass."

The mistake might have been upsetting if he hadn't smiled on Donatella's self-conscious descent.

Despina caught up with her sleeve. "See that breakfast is ready."

"I'm not hungry, just tired," Signor Stradella defied reports of being troublesome.

"Well, I could eat in my sleep." Golone looked for any reaction, struggling sideways up stair by stair. Maestro's eyes were down again, the harpsichord at his chest so with the sway of his head and posture of shoulders and arms he might play and carry it at the same time.

"They brought it all the way from Modena?" Donatella found Nubesta in the breakfast room where hard boiled eggs, fresh anchovies, and chickpea *polenta* wouldn't be wasted.

"No. The Strata Nuova."

"Why wasn't it delivered yesterday?"

"Signor insisted he handle it himself." Nubesta was thrilled with what she knew and Donatella didn't. "So you were a thief in the night."

"I didn't steal anything."

"That's not what I meant. But you did what you said you wouldn't."

"Well ... yes ... at his request."

"Bait."

"Ridiculous."

"You've never been hooked."

Donatella had been, then dangled and let go, almost before Nubesta was born.

"Well, I don't mind." Nubesta was eating, slumped on the couch beside double doors opened onto an orchid filled conservatory.

The young servant didn't appreciate the limits of her life, hungry for experiences as for the breakfast not meant for her. It wasn't that she was a bad girl—Despina wouldn't have her in the house if she were—but her restlessness seemed more unfortunate than her circumstances.

"We won't see much of him."

"Will he invite his ladies?"

Donatella didn't want to think let alone talk about such things. She wouldn't mind the continuo of a harpsichord stopping and starting as masterpieces were made, its vibrations inspiring the ornamentation of a violin. Soft sighs from a lute would be for the silence of the night when he couldn't dream without a respondent in his arms. That was how it would be with him there, the sublime above their heads, any scandal somewhere else. Nothing would be seen of him but coming and going, or known of his needs except what the ladies of the household could respectably fulfill.

"Should we take up a tray?" Donatella turned when Nubesta stood and swallowed.

Despina had come into the room. "No. Don't you listen? Signor is resting."

"Did he say anything about the apartment?"

"He shouldn't have any problem with it."

"Well, he seems easy to please."

Nubesta laughed like a woman twice her age.

Despina stood at the sideboard to eat or not, waving away flies deciding for her. "Get some netting to cover this."

The maid was gone, her heavy steps as obvious as her scowl.

"Close the shutters. The sun's already hot and will fade the carpet."

Donatella plunged the beginnings of the day into night as perhaps the new lodger had done. No, his rooms were on the west side, with windows for viewing ships and sunsets.

***

"Is he finally here?" Nonna let Donatella open the curtains where violets thrived on a north-facing water-marked windowsill.

"Yes, Nonna."

"And?"

Donatella brought over the basin.

"Tell me."

"He moved in." She sponged her grandmother's forehead, around her almond shaped eyes, sagging cheeks and bristled chin, and down her still supple neck.

"With a lot of commotion."

"It couldn't be helped," Donatella put the basin aside, "carrying a harpsichord upstairs."

"*L'oh*. Then I'll never see it or hear it."

"He also has a violin and three lutes." She smoothed Nonna's hair. "What would you like for breakfast?"

"You should copy for him."

"He must have someone already."

"You would do it better."

"I'd rather look after you."

"You're too sacrificing."

"You gave up singing."

"When it was no longer accompanied by *desidèrio*."

"But you still wanted to perform."

"For my ego, not *pubblico*." Nonna was tiring.

"Will you sit in the chair a while?"

"You should copy for him."

Was her grandmother forgetful or stubborn? "I'll bring you some breakfast? At least warm milk?"

"At least you took him some warm chocolate?"

"No. He traveled all night and needs to sleep."

"*Così*, he'll wake for dinner."

"We'll see."

"There's always supper."

"He'll probably go out."

"When he gets back, a slice of *torta di anice* to help his digestion. Especially if Despina is asleep."

Nubesta overheard. "She's looking for you."

"No wonder Julianna ran away." Nonna made the sign of the cross.

"Mama didn't." Donatella waved Nubesta out of the room. "She went with father."

There was no reply but the sinking of her grandmother's head into the pillows.

Nubesta was waiting. "Some problem in the apartment."

"Why? Didn't he like what was done?"

The girl shrugged with insinuation.

Even as Donatella climbed the stairs to the consequence of an offense that was obedience, she couldn't regret the experience of a life she would otherwise never know. Already it was over and done with, Signor Stradella turning away what he had invited, spoiled and hypocritical, too, for could an intruder be intruded upon? He might have just put things where and as he wanted, nothing else said about it. Of course, he was used to making dramas, setting scenes, and directing emotions, too often moved by illicit contracts and embezzlements, broken vows and hearts.

The light came after her as if the sky was below and she was on her way to somewhere less clear but more brilliant, especially while she heard keyboard music. Her stomach rolled. Suddenly there wasn't any doubt Signor Stradella was as entitled as presumptuous, in melody the master and lyric the servant, life a gamble, death convinced and cheated, talent the redeemer.

"Have you seen your room?" Her aunt's grating voice, even directed at Golone, caused Donatella discomfort.

"Fit for a servant."

"But not you, my man?" Signor Stradella smoothly intervened.

"Am I given a choice, Maestro?"

The harpsichord answered with a little humor in touch and tone.

"There you are. I don't know what you were thinking." Despina's heavy skirt was as threatening as her voice coming down.

Donatella reached her with a facial armor she had learned to have ready to wear.

"Look at you." Despina tugged her niece's chemise higher than her loosely laced bodice. "No wonder he mistook you for the maid."

"I'll go up."

Her aunt dropped her hands and bottom lip. "Whatever for?"

"I should apologize."

"I already did."

Donatella was also ashamed of her worn shoes that showed as she turned to avoid an unnecessary encounter.

"Well, will you not see the *crimine*?"

Signor Stradella leaned over the third floor balustrade, more likely to fly than jump.

"We'll take care of it at once, signor." Despina pushed her niece against the railing. "Nubesta!"

He conducted Donatella up like a note from a horn or soprano, then stroked back his hair and loosened his cravat, smiling more intentionally than when earlier she had stepped out of the way. She hypnotically moved in his direction, less nervous than curious, less curious than uncertain, less uncertain than hopeful this ascent wouldn't let her down. On the third floor she would have liked the assurance of his direct eyes and another word in his Roman accent, instead following the stride of his lithe body removing a long coat. As she walked into the apartment through one arched doorway and another, she was embarrassed—not only for being alone with him then but thinking she knew him before she did.

"*Grazie,*" Signor Stradella was reopening a window, "for such a *composizione idillica.*"

She felt compelled to admit her earlier irresponsibility as bells tolled, to hear them clearer and be refreshed by the dawning she couldn't yet see, a sweet draft yet another intruder meaning or not to leave something behind.

At least Signor Stradella pretended pleasure over the sticky blossoms littering the unpolished panels of floor and even out to the red and blue patterns of the rug in the center of the room.

"I'm sorry. I forgot to close it."

"Ah. It must be cleaned up," Stradella greeted Nubesta, her interruption not denying she had listened longer than it took her to come in.

"Like everything in this house." The girl bent over, hoping to be appreciated.

"My aunt wants things neat." Donatella had considered continuing her mistaken identity, but was afraid it would prove too convincing.

"*Scusi, signorina.* I should've realized." There was as much skill as sincerity in his apology and slight bow.

"That's right, I'm the maid." Nubesta was proud.

Dismissed, she left and Donatella suddenly felt a stranger to herself as well as to him, and unprepared to make that acquaintance, either.

CHAPTER THREE

The door closed. And Donatella was trapped rather than accused.

"*Così*, you unpacked my things?"

"Yes."

"I always welcome a woman's touch." He knew his effect, disappearing into the bedroom, a dream and yet as existent as a beggar on a street corner. "Ah. *Buon, buon*."

She shouldn't have followed him; such temptation was a stranger to her.

"You wonder why?" He turned from the bed having pulled its spread back. "*Certamente*, you've heard?"

Before her was a gracious creature, especially his hands composing in mid-air and eyes shifting slowly in observation and expression. His hair was an admission of the recklessness that got him in trouble, the vagrancy of his genius making him too accessible. Without music's influence he might not wander like a prince among his subjects, although who could think that was all there was to him?

"It's widely known," he sat on the bed untying his sleeves, pursing his lips in the same motion as a wink, "finer sheets bring me *difficoltà*."

If Donatella hadn't already seen his confidence and heard the tease of his voice, she might have been shocked, although behind her seeming composure was disappointment at being sent away so he could sleep. As soon as she was in her room, she pulled her cap off. She still had nice hair, long and waving as easily as it tangled, darkened honey with a few signs of gray. Her complexion was at its best out of doors, for years only up and down the slender garden behind the house and on Sundays a short veiled walk to church.

Even in unflattering clothing her figure was apparent, once at least something to blush for. Now self-consciousness was unnecessary, only her general attention required like an audience removed from the action.

Removed didn't mean unaffected, able to just walk away without considering what was seen and heard. So it was easier to believe what was heard and unseen when she was more dazzled than dazzling beside her grandmother in a mirrored hall, talk not only of an excellent opera and its reception but the composer and his past. He also had a reputation for lucky escapes: in *Roma* on the steps of *Santa Giovanni* where an oratorio inspired enough appreciation to thwart assassination, and in *Torino* where his wounds didn't stop him accepting an invitation to the carnival of the seaport often referred to as *la Superba.* If there was any doubt he deserved a reprieve, that evening of falling verse and *Genovese* paradox persuaded most into gratefulness, earning him more time and yet another place in redemption and risk.

***

The azalea flower was suggestive of the new lodger, with a passion for color itself, spraying out from its dramatic center like a cat's whiskers for effect and purpose, rising stealthily through the shade to reach for the wind as much as the sun. After a nap and persuading her grandmother to try a little broth, Donatella spent the afternoon where buzzing wisteria and honeysuckle blurred the angles of walls also stepping up with budding hibiscus and geraniums to larger terracotta pots of bay and lemon trees surrounding a sunny plateau. A city sky was more available there than in the street, flat baskets drying basil, a rusty ironwork table and several chairs reminding how lunch or supper used to be taken for granted.

She sat long enough to be covered in blossoms and catkins from a few trees in neighboring yards like boys grown too big for their breeches, what was pleasing also a source of unpleasantness. Her aunt would want her to sweep there, too; always for Donatella to be a poor relation. In Genoa, it was a matter of looking up or down; Despina was certainly its citizen. So was Donatella, accepting what was unacceptable, her interior life pretending to be better than it was, although Nonna blamed a tendency to *malinconia* on her granddaughter's English side with too much rain in her blood. As if climate could be inherited—shifting skies of clouds and sun, never warmer than it was still cool in the shade, hay growing and ripening despite wet feet, root vegetables the staple, walls and hedges rolling along landscapes far from the sea.

Donatella also liked hearing how an Oxfordshire grandfather always wore a flower, even in winter, and a red face—not for shame in his love of ale.

"There you are. What a mess those trees made here" Her aunt was predictable. "They should be cut down."

"No."

"Well, any overhanging branches at least. But if you keep the path neater I won't think about it."

When Despina had gone inside Donatella fetched the broom from the shed near the steps leading down to the cellar.

"Instead you could find me a flower." Signor Stradella proved he was a master of near misses as well as melody. "A return is a sort of encore and needs *ornamento*."

He had grown taller until Donatella realized it was the styling of his wig, the straight length of his blue velvet coat and buttoned vest, his legs posed in barely a glimpse of tasseled breeches but mostly unwrinkled hose of burnished gold, daring heels on his shoes. His positioning with one hand on his hip and the other in mid-air made him look like a *funzionario* claiming importance, but his pronouncement was a smile anyone would easily agree to.

"So what do you think?" he saw her choice before she made it. "Ah. *Perfetto*. The *colore* of the heart."

His ballooning sleeves twisted an azalea cluster into an also cumbersome cravat. All that creamy lace cascading down his breast accented by the bursting red of his heart was so pretentious she quietly laughed.

He did too, showing his teeth as he probably wouldn't in the company he was returning to, although there was a sense he didn't intend to live longer with them in mind. Or maybe it was just the truth when he said, "*Così*, there's no cause to flatter you."

She was offended and relieved, all further exchanges between them decided. He moved through the garden with the flirtatious restlessness of a butterfly.

"This is quaint. I must look ridiculous." He turned back, his shoulders lifting with the hope in his voice. That she wouldn't agree?

She tried to follow him without seeming overly forward. "Well, it's been some time since a gentleman walked here."

"I hope I haven't broken a spell. But what of Garibaldi?"

"He's mostly an absent landlord."

"Until he imposes a *fuggitivo* onto you."

"No, I see it," she chose her words carefully, "as a privilege."

"Ah," his modesty was less practiced than hers, "this constant tidying. *Ancora*, your aunt's wishes?"

"Well, yes."

"And yours?" He frowned like a child looking for another with which to misbehave. "You take care of this?"

"We're also tenants."

"I know. You should see the gardens of the *nobiltà*."

It was too soon to contradict his assumptions.

"They weep and tumble, propose and abandon, rising and falling in steps and sidesteps, plucking strings, sounding horns and peacocks, sweeping eyes and souls to the sea."

She found herself believing the sky was carrying accolades from God, refraining from gathering them up and offering them to him as he was ready to leave that insignificant stage.

"Golone! Am I late? I told you not to let me be late."

His servant stood in the conservatory entrance wiping his mouth with his sleeve. "I was hungry."

"Not merely the kitchen inviting."

Donatella noticed Nubesta standing behind him and that Golone wasn't bad-looking, round faced and deep eyed with dimples in his cheeks.

"After all, Maestro, I haven't appearances to keep."

"Then I might do without you?"

"Well, you might. But that would be refusing a gift."

"I've had more pleasing ones."

"And more dangerous."

"*Così*, though always late, with you I'm safe?"

It was obviously a banter they were used to without feeling any insult. Signor Stradella did show impatience for Golone to abandon Nubesta and brush his wig and coat. Donatella's hand was wiser than her disappointment when he didn't acknowledge what was resisted.

He couldn't avoid Despina wondering what time he would be back, Golone laughing and following his answer of rushing out.

"He'll soon be in trouble again."

Donatella had nothing to say about Signor Stradella until she sat with Nonna, only admitting she had watched him turn towards Genoa's piece of the sea. Her grandmother decided his destination was the *Casa Doria* or the *Palazzo Ducale,* the royal couple giving a dinner or ball in his honor, for a few hours allowing his music and celebrity to reign. So they would have the satisfaction of seeing him approved and improved under their influence, his most noted performances for public pleasure, whispers to the contrary never reaching their ears.

And Nonna—how did she know what there was no one to tell her of? She smiled with her own memories of entertaining such patronizing circles, eventually falling asleep breathing nasally.

Donatella adjusted the bed's pillows so Nonna's chin didn't fall against her chest, and shooed the cats away from the nightstand and a cup of milk otherwise barely touched. Sitting in the chair by the window she caught a breath from the bay through the side of the curtains, Caprice and Bianchi with nowhere to go but her lap and at her feet until the rug by the unlit hearth was a more settling choice. She wondered what it was like to walk into the ambivalent heart of the city, through its tangle of *carruggi,* risking life itself for the sudden fantasy of a buttery yellow and rose confection pillared and layered to replicate a doge's palace. Of course its façade was a cheap trick of art; not for everyone to taste the richness of its interior. Donatella also had Nonna's word on the easy swing of silk skirts over caramelized floors and the slide of a singer's hands along swirling balustrades, slowly but surely stepping up to the decadence of crystallized candles and golden glazed ancestors. So this approach was all dessert, culminating in pale chocolate and mint and creamy nougats carved out of truth and myth, no necessity of it until tasted, and then an endless craving.

Donatella didn't have pen and ink at hand or want to disturb the cats, but still could imagine Signor Stradella quite delicious himself in fashionable dress and closed smile, hardly discouraging a standing ovation just for the performance of his return. Which was icing on the cake of being so grandly welcomed rather than stewing in prison or rotting in a grave or worse still with no flavor at all. As he made his way to the marble dais, greetings reached out in hope of his reformation, the men behind viola and lute rising as excited as any lovers to have him back. His arms opened, waving the singer forward and kissing her hand, whether or not a goddess, showing her off like one. Until he flipped back his coat to sit at the white and gold harpsichord, taking his time, bowing his head, bending his arms and positioning his fingers.

He created silence as much as sound, in commissioned confessions, no man more desirable in appearance even as he mocked adulation, making beautiful music and mischief. For him it was all about persuasion, the choice of ruin or uncertain victory with the call to arms always a possibility. Of course it might be argued the words weren't his but even a goddess should be grateful for the power he gave her, syllabic composition collaborating with her vocal illustration, the motion of originality freeing her from the stiffness of recital. Otherwise she would be like the mythical statues around that room, decoration without any kind of presence.

"Sing, Stradella, sing," they shouted, although he certainly wasn't a *castrato* and the soprano was prepared for an encore.

He deferred to her, bringing her forward and begging her to perform again but she left the stage with grace if little dignity.

"Sing!"

Refusal was still an option, but he remembered to be favored and looked for the prince or princess, the latter making the most of the opportunity and her jewels by lifting her hands as if offering alms. He nodded, bending towards the other musicians and facing his future of obliging not only for bread and butter but also the occasional dessert.

***

Donatella tried not to be obvious, waiting for the warning of the front door and loud heels.

"Why don't you come and read to me?" her aunt found her. "You do it so well."

"Not tonight."

Despina couldn't be trusted to be conciliatory. "His affairs aren't ours."

"I know." Donatella wouldn't agree more, following her into the hallway. "I'm going to bed. I want to be up for market."

"You never go."

"I used to. With Mama."

"It was—is— not respectable."

"What's this I hear?" A voice was still in full song, its owner lightly ascending to join them under whitewashed cross-vaulting and a dangling cluster of candles.

"Signor. How did you get in?"

"The maid," he glanced towards Donatella, "at the side door."

"Oh, you haven't lost your key already?"

He held it up, intricately filigreed and recently polished. "Well, it was Golone, really, when he saw a *nuovo amore* in the alley. And I haven't had to sneak around for a while."

Donatella couldn't help but approve of a man who dressed for a palace to walk in an ordinary garden, through narrow twisted alleys, even using the servant's entrance, as though his triumph wasn't in the expense of clothes or distinction of patrons, the shine in his eyes only partly due to the generosity of fine wine and equally intoxicating ladies.

CHAPTER FOUR

She was barely awake. No sooner had Donatella headed towards Genoa's still dark piece of the sea, Nubesta caught up with her and took the marketing basket.

"You can't go alone."

"You do. And you're pretty."

Nubesta liked flattery, but not giving up an hour or so of freedom. "Your aunt will be angry."

"Of course." The girl looked back to the house, quickening her steps until she was leading, her coarse brown sleeves pushed to her elbows. Hurrying might explain her uncovered hair straying from its braid onto the bareness of her neck, the shawl collar slipped because it hadn't been fixed tight enough, either.

Donatella was uncomfortably obedient, in a long black cloak according to the recent *prammatica.* "I've almost forgotten the way, it's been so long."

"My legs know even if my head's still sleepy." Nubesta slowed and reached for Donatella's hand.

It was an improper gesture. But why should they be appropriate or inhibited or forever in mourning? Why should Genoa? Because its roofs were grey instead of red, eyes downcast, and power nothing like the sea's? Mistress and maid were conjoined like the city, everything up against everything else along streets without a sky. Yet somehow sun and stars splashed its layers, domes and towers distinguished by nature and man, plain living brightening into columned courtyards and sculptured edifices, fronts not as simple as black and white. Further apart in age than importance, Donatella and Nubesta characterized Genoa's contradictions and blend, modesty and posturing, poverty and prosperity, experience and imagination, sharing what was separate. Especially Donatella, who had lived large and small, been brought up and down.

The early morning was quiet until the square was full. *Mercato dei Banchi* stirred saints and sinners to its common purpose of supply and demand under the influence of a church-spired crown and weathered frescos, alternatives for salvation in the money changers hall. Nubesta whispered a warning of pickpockets on both sides, the *Chiesa di San Pietro* irrelevant to the loitering around its subsidy of shops selling local metalwork, lace, and velvet draperies. They lingered until seen to be more interested than they could afford, escaping with unexplained guilt to the square's tumbling fruits and vegetables, flowers growing from buckets and soliciting hands, baked goods and herbs mingling with the flavor of garlic and seafood still appealing in the dawn's coolness.

Nubesta was easily dismissed to the attention of a sea-swept face behind one of the fish stalls, Donatella moving on to cheese and the large woman surrounded by helpful children offering samples. She tasted the sharpest and bought the mildest along with a jar of mushroom and potato tripe the seller boasted of. Further along the row she decided on a round bread loaf, plain *focaccia,* and finally a pastry filled with vanilla and pistachio cream she insisted be wrapped separately.

Nubesta was where and as she had left her, choosing flattery over fish. The girl smiled without apology. "I was waiting to see what you wanted."

"You know."

"Thought maybe something different."

"No. Dried mackerel, mussels, *calamari,* and cheap but fresh fish."

"Stew again?"

"What the budget allows."

"And if Signor Stradella eats with us?"

"He'll eat fish stew."

The boy splattered with pale blood continued to enjoy Nubesta's boldness, Donatella handing over all the packages but one.

"Where are you going?"

"Never mind. Wait for me here."

Donatella walked away, going back patiently, hopelessly, knowing the view and yet seeing it differently, down to the unchanging basin and wharf with an interest in the sea which for her was gone except for sunsets and stew. She passed through the shipper's square overlooked by the palatial *Banco San Giorgio* representing the whole city looking out to sea with its back to the mountains. Its painted face was still in night's shadow, not for shame but profitability of any workings inside. The first activity of the quay was a few stygian fishermen returning with squeaky barrows and splintery baskets emptied at market. Some stopped to talk, perhaps about the woman in a shroud without the attitude for it. Donatella would have preferred to enjoy her treat unremarkably and watch another day shed its light on the bay if nothing else. The best she could do was take refuge behind an old man repairing a net cascading from a frame and over his knees, his eyes only for its impressive knotting—and the pastry she unwrapped, stepping close enough to offer him half.

He took it with a hand as cut and dried as the words she couldn't comprehend but wanted to remember. If Genoese was strange, although she had always lived in its home, another language coming from somewhere else was familiar. There was an English ship in port, identified by its high-flying standard but also strong masts and newly varnished hull, as long and unapproachable as the years since she had stepped off shore.

Long ago but not far from there she had walked with her only suitor, trying to understand everything he told her, like the sea's people being much the same the world over. It wasn't so unbelievable he had seen the whole world when he smiled, squeezed her shoulders, and looked as if he knew what would come next.

The fisherman was folding his net and singing dissonantly, prayer-like, with something of the torment and comfort of waves crashing against the *ripa*. What would Maestro Stradella have made of such unbeautiful music as suggestive of an impending disaster as Golone approaching with Nubesta, carrying her basket and holding her hand?

"I need to buy ink," he said in response to the maid's reluctance to take back either. "He scribbled all night and ran out."

Donatella suspected Golone wasn't honorable, more because he used too much musk oil than that he served a wandering master. "He works through the night?"

"When there's a deadline."

"And you stay up with him?"

"Only if drinking is involved."

Nubesta was picking something and nothing off his sleeve, Donatella also finding any excuse to look away. The fisherman's talents of making nets and songs were gone, but the bay's sky was brightening, unlike

Nubesta's face when Golone continued on his mission of buying ink and some time for himself.

I didn't think you'd have hopes there, Donatella might've told Nubesta as the Captain had said to her. Other girls had fathers with titles and schemes that weren't about voyages but settling, especially on dowries. Donatella's was just more adventurous, ignoring his daughter's heart, sailing away with the risk she was almost willing to take. Once she never wanted to see him again, large, strong, decorated and silver-wigged, with hands that didn't need to move when he struggled with a foreign language and emotion.

"It's for the good."

"No one stopped you and Mama."

"Not for the good."

"You don't mean that."

They hadn't tried to discuss it further, Despina catching them in a silence implying something unseemly was going on.

"Nonna tells me she's taking Donatella to the theater."

The Captain, shaking his head, had at least understood Despina was as curious as disapproving.

"I think, just the diversion I need, Papa."

"My dear girl. For the right associations?"

"Does it matter, Aunt?"

"Or just to forget the wrong ones?"

The Captain had turned towards the sound of Nonna rehearsing with hands and voice.

"My mother sings, in public. And married a charlatan I'm ashamed was my father."

Despina should have spoken slower, but somehow the Captain had a mispronounced answer.

"Well, sister-in-law, you could not be so foolish."

***

With Despina resentments were long lived; she always needed someone to be angry at. When Donatella and Nubesta got back to the house she hadn't even washed Nonna's face, another punishment of her niece for taking to the streets.

"She might care more for her own mother," Nubesta scolded.

Donatella agreed, although not with the maid's impertinence. "Why are you up here? Where's the basket?"

Nubesta shrugged and pointed to the bottom of the stairs.

"Well, bring it to the kitchen."

Despina got there first, shoving the shopping at Nubesta while addressing her niece's sudden adventurousness. "So what did you get?"

"Fish for stew." Nubesta wrinkled her nose.

Donatella almost smiled but knew it would be wiser to get on with taking care of Nonna who made too much of *il maestro* living with them, helping to hang out the washing in the shadows sloping up from the scullery, and chopping carrots and onions for the *buridda*. Cook was regretfully interested in the trip to market, her legs too old to take her so far anymore.

Donatella tried to speak as the old fisherman had.

"What?" Cook needed to hear it again. "It's an old proverb."

But *you cannot sip and breathe at the same time* hardly translated into something meaningful.

Golone came in through the alleyway and Nubesta dropped the pan she was washing, eager to greet him. He held up a small parcel, then ran out of the kitchen and up the stairs two at a time. The girl couldn't follow him but Donatella did, as far as she had any reason to go. In her room she listened to the flap of laundry from that house and others, her disheveled appearance reflecting the same reality. She felt tired of being a drudge and clothed like mid-winter, slowly and unsurely changing into a light blue frock that lengthened her neck, letting down one strand of hair she curled around a finger.

***

"Donatella? Is that you?"

She saw the light in her grandmother's room, something more than late morning allowed in.

"Come quickly."

Just as Donatella panicked she heard careful laughter, like in the days of easy steps and smiles, her grandmother's voice better than *Centoventi's* because it didn't listen to itself.

"There you are."

"Nonna, are you ... oh."

A willow of a man was bent over from the chair pulled near the bed, half-dressed in shirt, breeches, and slippers. His upper body and arms flowed towards Nonna, his face slowly emerging from a mask of hair with the weariness of being middle-aged and missing sleep, but also with the satisfaction of what had been accomplished.

"And who's this, *cara signora*? You didn't say you had another granddaughter."

"Only one. And she is too modest about the talent she has with brush and pen."

"A budding Artemisia Gentileschi." He turned the pages of Donatella's journal with an empathy one artist shows another.

"Nothing so important. Just about flowers."

"Come here," Nonna pleaded as Donatella could never refuse. "Look, *signore,* at the beauty in her."

Donatella was aware of smelling like onions as Nonna put her hands in his.

"*Maestro,* here is your copyist."

PART TWO

The Arrangement

CHAPTER FIVE

She began carefully. Still a mistake happened on the last note, blotted with her handkerchief and lightly scraped at the tip of a clean quill, re-formed and powdered, just a hint of correction on the parchment. She had spent the entire afternoon on one page and thanked the Madonna it wasn't spoiled. Working off the original, hearing music as it had yet to be played, she did her best to imitate its autograph of leaps and twirls and tidy unfinished marks and changes made in the rush of inspiration.

She wanted to show ability beyond the ladylike diversion of scribbling thoughts or painting in a journal, obsessing over the responsibility for something greater than nothing better to do.

Bad light was a consequence of secrecy, such occupation, like the corner of her room, not meant for illumination. At least it was no longer necessary to deceive rather than disappoint Nonna. Signor Stradella might have appreciated the steadiness and unsteadiness of Donatella's hand, but the idea of it working for him was also indulged and dropped—until Golone delivered a message tied with blue satin ribbon and smelling of jasmine because there was a sprig in its knot.

Donatella unrolled it out of sight where the persuasive fragrance and request could be enjoyed, barely resisting a hasty reply.

A few hours after she put it into Golone's hands, Nubesta found her reading to Nonna. Donatella closed the book that had almost lulled her to sleep, too.

"*Maestro*." Nonna tried to sit up. "He wants you to continue. Don't think about it. He is waiting."

"No, it's Golone." Nubesta pulled him in. "To continue what?"

Donatella approached him for a well-worn folder with papers inserted every which way, a bundle of quills and a large jar of ink turning her into a juggler.

"He wondered where you'll work."

"Where," she was afraid her grandmother had heard, "I do now."

Golone wasn't any more alert. "You might use his apartment."

"Despina won't allow it." Nonna saved her from not knowing what to answer.

He shrugged, a servant to impropriety, and followed Nubesta out.

Although Donatella didn't go to Signor Stradella's apartment or see him except in passing, eventually she had to meet his approval.

Nonna had taught her to read music, not rudimentarily but with imagination, like seeing branches designed for the sky as well as the tree. She remembered her grandmother's complaints about a page ending in the worse place for turning and notation that was too silent. As the written word should be heard but not spoken, music should speak before being heard. It was half a week before Donatella embellished the heading to finish: *Per un barcheggio, 8 Giugno, 1681*. In her eye's opinion she had added neatness to fluency, expecting suggestions, but satisfied.

She laid her copy of the aria on the bed, stepping back.

Nonna called singing her *lavoro,* in those days *radicale* and hardly suitable now. When had Donatella thought of work except as there were too few servants to run the house and her aunt made her seem one of them? Anything else was idleness, whether reading, gardening, or prettiness with the needle, on a keyboard, in painting or slips of verse no longer seen as accomplishments.

It was a Sunday morning when she tried to return the folder with the copy included. Golone wouldn't have it, leaving the house in a hurry.

She might take advantage of Nubesta's day off, as well, if Signor Stradella returned directly from whatever service his music attended while Despina napped after going to mass. Donatella trailed her aunt down small streets and across the square named for the closest church open to her faith even when she had none. For once she wished she wasn't late. *Santa Maria Maddalena* was filled with music as sacred as its interior; a modest congregation settling amid its garlanded pillars and gilded moldings, nearer to heaven anticipated in the ceiling of the main altar. Her aunt looked for her to slide into their usual pew but Donatella's skirt didn't completely leave the aisle and she ignored a whispered objection more adamant as heads turned, putting herself forward as she never did except for communion.

It wasn't her intention to be seen reverent in the ritual of silk and linen vestments and covers, golden chalice, paten and tall tapers, or kneeling nearer the graceful pain of the crucifixion, to be overheard less than fluent in echoes of Latin. She sat back and it was obvious why she was there: not for the usual madrigalists shielding the altar and taking direction from the pulpit, but an almost heretical performance in the small gilded gallery to her left, a stone rolled away, resurrection in the pleasured expression of strings and a man to whom every passion was necessary.

It wasn't the place for bows except in prayer. Signor Stradella's attention soon moved to the young lady by his side who had sung with sweetness, not strength.

On the way home one of the better houses was inviting. Despina sent her niece on, Donatella only minding the weight of her veil and skirt in the May shower that wasn't unexpected either.

"Artemisia."

She didn't turn around.

By the time she hurried across the *via Luccoli* to face Saint George and the courage she lacked, the pavement was steaming and her resolve changing as quickly as the weather. Signor Stradella pushed the gate for her to go first, his rain-scented shrewdness surrounding her as he opened the front door.

"My aunt will be home soon."

"Ah. We have a secret." He slid his violin case from under his coat.

At least they weren't alone in the house, Cook singing without Despina there to mind, and Nonna calling. He tapped Donatella's arm and asked how the assignment was coming along.

"It's finished."

"*Bravissima*. Let me see."

"We could use the breakfast room."

"Or less *prudenza*."

Nonna just wanted to know she was back. "And *Signore Stradella*?"

"I haven't seen him today."

"I think you have."

"Well, for a moment—"

"In the rain?"

"Oh. I should change."

"No. You look as you must," her grandmother smacked her lips, "caught off guard."

Besides the folder of music, Donatella carried up a tray of *limonata* and anise cake, another of Nonna's suggestions.

"At last."

She smelled a candle burning, but it didn't light the short hall. In the main room a window was open, with the settee moved closer to it, Signor Stradella a masterpiece resting there. One dark leg was stretched and falling over the back of the couch, a ruffled hand on its knee; the other bent to the floor and, even without stocking and shoe, appeared ready to walk away. He had also undressed to his shirt still buttoned high and wrinkled softly because it was made of the finest linen. A slight breeze blew his hair over his face. As he realized her burdened entrance, his right shoulder pillowed a half-smile and he reached out lazily.

"Did you bring *bavareisa*?"

"What's that?" She clumsily laid the tray down on the gray marble hearth, not wanting to bend with her back to him.

"*Cioccolata* and *caffè*."

"We don't have coffee. It's too expensive."

"I'll pay for it." He swung into sitting, hunched and rubbing his neck. "I'm getting one of my headaches."

"It's the weather." Donatella offered him a drink.

He accepted it, the tips of his fingers friendlier than they should have been. "A veil over the sun, like a woman at *Messa*." He tasted it. "Ah. *Fresco*."

"Squeezed this morning. Nonna says it's good for clearing the voice."

"*Cara Nònna*." He raised his glass, then emptied it with a kiss on its rim. "I've heard she was very rebellious. I wonder you didn't become the same."

"I wasn't meant to."

"How do you know?"

"Because it didn't happen."

She was still holding the folder.

"I believe that's why you've come?"

He moved slowly to make space on the table where his inventions were layered and sprawled, so many at once. By the time she placed the copy there he was sitting once more, leaning forward, his head in his hands.

"You can let me know." She felt intrusive. "I've never seen you at Maddalena before."

He rose, admitting his rudeness. "I was testing the sound for a wedding there."

"It must be a special one."

"Ah. I'll make it so." His teeth showed. "*Così.*" He leaned over the table, the side of his face long and angled, eyelashes still and mouth taut, the first page flipped for the second, the second for the third, every one after that as unremarkable.

"I'm untrained."

He looked at the first page again, his index finger, chin, and muted hum following the stanzas. "Ah. You see. Just a little more space here and this note a little higher, the words not quite aligned."

Her hope of impressing him was gone.

"No, no." He showed sensitivity to being misunderstood. "Even my last copyist, a priest, cursed my sloppiness."

"I did my best."

"Ah. Anyway, there are many *arie* in the *serenata*, besides *duetti* and *trii* and *sinfonie*. I need copies of each by—you saw the date; barely a month away. Before that for rehearsal." He closed the folder, falling back on the settee. "And only so-called *musicisti* in *Genova*, too quick or too slow or distracted by *ambizione*. Will you do more for me?"

She had to consider. His reputation. Her motivation. She couldn't sign her name to the work, freely spend any payment, or even show some pride. Sneaking around, her aunt would eventually find out and put a stop to it anyway.

"Is that cake?"

"Yes."

"For the flies?"

"Oh." She rescued the plate.

He took a slice, eating it almost without chewing. "As we live dangerously opening windows."

He reached for another, nodding for her to take what was left.

"All right," she answered.

"*Bene allora.*"

"I mean ... I will help you."

"*Mangia.*"

"Oh, yes." She broke a corner of the last piece on the plate.

He got up to pour her a glass of *limonata,* staring as her lips, covered in crumbs, finally took a sip.

CHAPTER SIX

She hadn't much time. Until the eighth of June was a deadline through its morning only, four festive galleys already in port, smaller boats gathering the night before with lanterns swaying in unheeded winds and displaying their own regalia. The barges were due to be pulled in and lined up around four in the afternoon so the silks for transforming them into a grand hall wouldn't fade in the sun that after all didn't even brighten the clouds. A week earlier, at Despina's invitation to lunch and numerous glasses of wine, Signor Stradella explained the plan for this *divertissement* in the bay by drawing little pictures and witticisms from a perverse sense of what made him a living.

Donatella was more impressed by him writing slower than he scratched out, biting his hand and grabbing his hair, throwing back his head and closing his eyes. He hadn't shaved or buttoned his shirt and didn't seem to remember he had sent for her.

"*Tromba* or *cornetta*?"

She assumed he was speaking to Golone, who set out his clothes for the evening and left with a smile that knew what would never happen.

"I told them to decide." He stood stiffly as she moved into the untidy salon. "But still they ask."

"What's the difference?"

It was as if she had thrown water on him. He shuddered, his back arched even before he sat at the harpsichord to play barely broken chords like a boat rolling on little trills of foam.

He motioned her over. "You copied by hand, now voice."

"Oh, no."

"*Sì*, sing. With me. One breath." His fingers were moving again, his voice letting hers lead, for courtesy and because she couldn't outperform him.

"And so you played the *tromba*."

"It felt like drowning might."

He slapped his thighs. "There are too many phrases like that. Why do I make it so *difficile*?"

She wouldn't guess.

"Hmm?" He played the trumpet line again, trying and refusing to break it into something easier and less wonderful. "If only there was more talent in *Genova*."

The mirror now above the console table was as elegant as she wasn't, her hair less carefully arranged than Nubesta's, the lace around her neck that might have improved her needing to be washed and starched. She looked tired from weeks of candles being excessively burned—her hands, too, blistered from the lye soap normally avoided with a long stick in the laundry coppers but desperately used to scrub off stains that had grown beyond her use of quill and ink for writing in a journal.

"What did you want me for?"

He went back to the table, offering some pages. "This *duetto*. It seems *soprano* and *basso* won't share a copy. Like a bed."

She couldn't hide her embarrassment as she reached out.

"Oh, you haven't taken care." He didn't exactly caress her hands, or merely examine them, either.

"It looks worse than—"

"*Olio d'oliva.* Cooled. Rub it on gently."

She stiffened as he showed her.

"*Certamente,* I don't mean to make you suffer."

"But how do you clean the ink off?"

He presented his stained fingers.

"You don't have to hide what you do."

"Except with the direction of my eyes?"

She picked up her next assignment, feeling unworthy of his gaze.

"*Presto*? There's not much time."

Sleep could never be more important. "I'll try."

He came after her waving a white flag. "Make a collar of this."

"I can't take it."

"You don't." Her shoulders were surrounded with his attention and fine lace cravat. "I give it."

***

On the day of *il Barcheggio* Signor Stradella was an unusual sight dressed and flying down the stairs just after eight in the morning, mumbling words no gentleman would. Or so Despina accused when he didn't close the gate behind him. Nonna assured that the *prammatica* would be lifted for the occasion, so Donatella washed her hair, pressed her new collar and considered what flower she might pin on it. Nubesta hoped to meet up with Golone who, even laden with his master's change of costume, blew her a kiss on his way out.

The first thunder cracked as Donatella was packing a basket of refreshments, Nubesta running to get the laundry in. They were still hanging it around the kitchen when Golone returned, consoled a little by Nubesta's readiness to help put his master's concert clothes upstairs. Instead, Despina sent the girl into the rain for candles.

"I thought we had a good supply," Despina considered who she should suspect.

"Ah, *signorina,* accuse me."

Signor Stradella triumphantly stepped down into the kitchen. He shook the wet out of his hair, removed his coat, which Cook held closer and longer than it took to hook near the fire, and sat at the salt-scrubbed table.

"What will happen?" Donatella looked for some sign of distress.

"*Nièntel Posposto.*" He motioned to Cook again, "What's there to eat?"

"You seem pleased," Despina said, also to Cook who was still over-attending to him.

"My prayers were answered."

"You wanted it to rain?"

"I need more time."

"Then use what you have wisely." Golone came in and assumed a place next to him.

Donatella hoped they wouldn't noticc hcr holding back tears for whal was happening that day. Signor Stradella enjoyed a bowl of broth as though he had never eaten at a better table, laughing at Golone's drooling, and breaking off a steamy piece of bread, complementing Cook with his mouth full. He was amused, not unkindly, when Despina, leaving, almost tripped over the cats who had decided the kitchen was where they should be.

They rubbed the men's legs, as enticing as enticed by oyster stock that eventually found a second table on the floor.

"You break rules without me." Nubesta returned sooner than she could have bought candles, immediately sitting on Golone's lap. Signor Stradella fed her bread and olives, the cats not missing his attention as they licked at their own scrounged meal.

Nubesta noticed Donatella's disapproval. "Go on. Say it."

"I will." Signor Stradella turned towards Donatella. "There's work to do."

"More copies?" she forgot who might be listening.

"I wondered what you'd been up to." Nubesta ignored Golone's mouth on her neck for Signor Stradella lifting her hand.

"You mustn't tell," he hardly pleaded.

"That you adore me?"

Golone squeezed her. "How foolish you are." Then he pushed her away.

Signor Stradella caught her so she had to stand when he did.

***

It was like starting all over again, revisions and even cast changes, copies misplaced and mistreated, and a whole section added an emerging tenor would never learn in time. Nonna insisted she didn't mind being neglected while Donatella was called to serve a master greater than conscience. That Despina didn't question her niece's disappearances may have been due to Nonna's clever admission of Donatella's preoccupation ... with painting.

"Better than her being bored or depressed."

"Bored? I'm never bored."

"*Naturalmente* not, Despina, you always have an interest in yourself."

"Well, you can't expect me to sit with you for hours."

"I'd rather you didn't."

When Donatella told Signor Stradella what she had overheard he proclaimed *adorazione* for her grandmother with a mind to run away with her *immediatamente* so others could enjoy the scandal, too. It was one of his few allusions to the past that had made him what he was and wasn't, fact and fiction creating his successes and failures.

On the sixteenth of June powder was blown across the last page of the last copy. Donatella put on an indifferent face, straw hat and gardening gloves, going from candle to sun light, deadheading flowers before they went to seed, clipping herbs before they flowered and laying them out to dry, picking lemons for a *limonata* steeped with fresh parsley.

"Just the way I like it," Nonna pretended patience to first enjoy the drink Donatella brought her, but couldn't wait to address her granddaughter's mood. "*Così*, what's wrong?"

"I feel useless again."

"Before long you will have more copying to do. I've spoken to Sandro."

"Sandro? Such familiarity? "

"*Bene*, if we are to elope."

Donatella had to smile.

"That's better."

"Oh, Nonna, even if you could … you wouldn't."

"*Cara mia.* He's an easy man," Nonna almost fell out of bed to pinch Donatella's cheek, "except to refuse."

Donatella knew what she meant when Signor Stradella asked her to assist him in public. If only she hadn't over-eaten *focaccia*, scorched her neck rearranging the pots on the terrace, thrown out the cosmetics idle on her dressing table for so long, or lost interest in styling her hair. Her sudden and long-lasting headache saved him from realizing how ill at ease she would be in a crowd of pleated taffetas and silks, small waists, tight ringlets, and bold gemstones and glances.

Nubesta complained she was left behind.

"Go up to Golone's room," Donatella wondered if she needed to tell her, "for I believe there will be fireworks later."

"You must be disappointed."

Donatella understood Nubesta's frustration. "Maybe you could get away."

Half an hour later her aunt's long face, ludicrously eye-lined and rosy-cheeked, looked in. "You might have gone with me," she dismissed the possibility of Donatella joining the celebration in more than a ride around the bay.

Signor Stradella had said to leave it to him, for didn't he know how to steal a lady away?

"Not with forgiving consequences," Nonna had reminded.

That was when Donatella's headache began. Despite feeling unwell, she did try to experience some of the concert in the bay from Golone's slanting window, Nubesta taking her other advice. The sunset was low, wide, and dramatically colored like a contest of dresses, the bay growing smaller into a harbor-side of dancing lights. Fireworks startled the sky, the horn of the *Lanterna* reminding of the sea's dissonance while stars were harmonically arranged like countless notes she was glad to hear before they sounded far and faintly away.

She heard scratching; it was unusual for her cats to be above the first floor. Despina didn't allow it, but what worried Donatella most was that they seemed to be urgently summoning her.

***

"Oh, my *nipote*. Are you better?"

"A little, Nonna. Are you all right?"

"No."

"What's wrong?"

"I'm heartsick."

"Do you need the doctor?"

"A *miracolo*."

"Why?"

Her grandmother looked pained again. "To leave you happier."

She was sleeping by the time Despina returned flushed and loud.

"Shhh," Donatella confronted her aunt.

"What an event, the best Genoa could offer!"

"I'm going to bed."

"Don't you want to know?"

"Tomorrow."

"Our galley was the closest so we saw the guests arrive, heard them introduced; we had some of the feast sent over and of course there was wonderful music."

"Yes."

"That's caught your interest. Everyone was impressed. Composed in my house, I told them." Despina knew her niece would never have boasted. "You heard the fireworks?"

"And saw them."

"Not like reflected on the bay. I might've let you come. Where's Nubesta?"

Donatella didn't think the girl was back yet. "Asleep. I'll help you undress."

"You're no good at it. I'll do it myself."

"Yes."

"You look awful." Her aunt thought of something else. "The ovation went on fifteen minutes."

"Were there sonnets?"

"Sonnets? You mean recited? I don't know." Despina didn't have that memory. "No matter. I'm sure it was better than that."

CHAPTER SEVEN

There wasn't a hint from above. Not the moan of a floorboard or missing maestro, the next morning also filled with the absence of celebration and any explanation why. Just before noon Golone went up with *biscotti* and coffee, soon coming down with a verdict.

"The music was magnificent but how the man is wasted."

That floating hall must have been grand, the evening impressive like its guests and food and music. In the glow Signor Stradella would have seemed an extraordinary success fitting brocaded silk, tilting crowning curls, his hands boasting gold set diamonds, his ambitions rising and bowing to the occasion.

But the day after was for remembering he would have to prove himself again.

In the shadows he was half-dressed, unwashed and uncertain. His smile might court admiration but Donatella had seen his defenses, glances more irritated than inviting, greasy hair and as uncontrolled moods hanging over the work he feared would never reveal the slowing of his heart. He was a property, noble and habitable like the house near *Luccoli*, for lease but not owning, skeletons in its closets, his often spoke of. Genoa had invited him with its voice of contradiction, to save and savor him, its leading gentlemen contending for him to visit, even stay in their homes with sisters, wives, and daughters faithfully hospitable. *Carnevale* was made for him; churches overlooked the sins of his appeal to the advantage of theirs. Signor Garibaldi and others put him in charge of the theater as long as his secrets were told in staged voices, movements as well directed and desires fulfilled for public pleasure.

"This came for Signor." Donatella closed the front door after the delivery of a letter. "It looks important."

Her aunt tried to take it; Donatella lifted it away from her. "I don't mean to read it."

Donatella was already on the stairs so she wouldn't see any objection.

She still wasn't comfortable going into Signor Stradella's apartment. Usually it was unlocked, the door ajar. Always there was anticipation, often the smell of coffee or tobacco, sometimes the music of the violin or harpsichord, even singing.

Now it was shut and silent.

She spoke to Golone, who was coming down from his room, tucking his shirt into his breeches.

"I brought up a letter."

"I'll take it."

"I slipped it under the door."

"A love note, then?"

"If so, from another."

Golone entered the apartment, bending over. "Good evening, Maestro. How's your head and gut? There's something for you. To make you feel better or worse? No, not from public security. They don't send such pretty things. Ah, the seal of Brignole. Expressing his pleasure, no doubt. But has he paid you anything yet?"

The reply wasn't for Donatella. She went downstairs to attend to her own business, soon reminded of Signor Stradella's impulses by what was fading in her grandmother's eyes: such resolve to reach for the highest notes and hopes and lovers, Nonna always proud to have her share. He was right; Donatella was so unlike her.

I believed and waited, for everything and nothing. I embraced the invisible as it embraced me. I learned to be very silent and still in this world of apparitions, not allowed to speak to anyone, just catch their breath and move out of their way.

Nonna sighed. "You write so regretfully. What do you regret?"

Donatella needed the words to be released from their privacy, yet the moment they were she was more of a prisoner to their meaning.

"I won't tell you to be careful."

"Then," Donatella put her journal and any weakening aside, "I'll listen to what you don't say."

***

Signor Stradella's revival heralded the next morning, like birdsong long past dawn, singing and playing scales on the harpsichord. Golone delivered a jug of hot water for him to wash; Nubesta returned from market with possibilities he leaned out a window for. Despina admonished the girl's playful reply, for what would the neighbors think? In the spirit of conciliation he joined Despina in the breakfast room, then, to amuse himself, looked in on and flirted with Nonna and for what indelicacies Cook had to offer. Donatella saw him leave the house mid-afternoon, before she sat in the garden attempting to paint shriveling flowers and dulling greens.

She skipped supper, pretending she had a headache again.

"Well, I told you not to stay in the sun so long," Despina was triumphant.

Later Donatella sank into English melancholy and the high backed chair, her cats purring *basso continuo* at her feet, Nonna sadly watchful.

"Go to bed. Perhaps you can still dream there."

Donatella kissed her and went downstairs to make sure the front door was locked, not knowing whether she had missed their tenant's return or if it was yet to happen. It seemed everyone had gone to bed, the kitchen fire smoldering, first floor rooms dark except for a little moonlight pervading the conservatory as sunlight would in half a dozen hours.

"*Signorina.* It's cooler here."

Her investigation into the garden was startled but not surprised.

"Have you ever slept outdoors?"

"No." She didn't visually identify who had spoken until she climbed up to the terrace where Signor Stradella was waiting. "Have you?"

"As a boy. I'd run away at night."

"Were you so unhappy?"

"No." He stood to pull out the other chair, moving it very close to his.

She sat. "Were you punished?"

"Like a cat with a saucer of milk."

"Then spoiled."

He seemed unusually embarrassed, but recovered quickly. "I never minded."

"Who would?"

"Those who expect *punizione*?" He saw she understood him. "Anyway, I remember the smell of the night, the possibilities for *vita* and *morte*, but especially the *immaginazione,* turning me into a stargazer and wanderer until I was ready for breakfast."

"I rarely go out after dark. Not even into the garden."

"So I spoil you, too." He smoothed a little of her skirt over his legs.

"Oh." She looked up at the house.

"Ah."

"I don't want her to see."

"See what?"

"Nothing." She tried to take back her skirt.

"You needed some air." He shifted, putting a decent space between them. "The boating night was even hotter. Wise you didn't come."

"It was?"

"*Così*. Your headache was an excuse."

"No."

"*Cara Nònna* thought so."

"You didn't?"

"A ploy. So I would have to tell you about it."

"I hoped so."

He smiled at her honesty and stood to tell his tale. "In the bay there was no limit to *Genovese* showing off, shared with every curious civilian like the sunset painting a backdrop to the parade shaping the *porto* out as far as the *Lanterna* and back to where most like your aunt weren't welcomed aboard the hall of barges. The construction was at first as impressive as its company in silk and ornaments and flowers, soon too warm for fashionable wigs and not seaworthy for heels and top heavy trestles of food. Large layered skirts concealed the spread of feet, made-up faces masked any nausea while gloves refined the drinking and fanning that could have been seen as coarse and flirtatious. So it wasn't just the floating hall that swayed the *signori* familiarly close to the *belle signore* they did and didn't apologize to.

"The flat boats rocked, the guests wouldn't be seated, and everyone and everything sweated. For one reason and another, the servers were frustrated and most attentive to swarms of flies landing on the *festa*. It was a ridiculous evening.

"Then my *musica* began. A mixture of harmonious voices, poetry and fine instrumentalists," Signor Stradella read from his palms, "a *signor importante* wrote."

"The letter that came?"

He lifted his hands in a question of his own but didn't hesitate to admit the singers were exceptional, as they should be, undertaking the instruction of not only notes but subtle interpretations. *Adagio, presto, mezzo tempo, allegro assai staccato, adagio e staccato, adagio forte e staccato, presto e staccato*. "I must've driven them mad with my demands—and not just the singers.

"The *tromboni* had to play rather *staccato* and with little breath like a dying man for a last word. It all took place on the center barge left open to the skies, settling stomachs, steadying gazes and silencing small talk. I stood up to the challenge, as cowardly as brave, with sea legs on land, sailing from one city to another, almost going down, buoyant again, even against the wrath of the gods. Let *Anfritrite* be jealous that she and *Nettuno* weren't the only lovers ruling the sea that night, such depth of *musica* in her whistles and hisses and whirlwinds. But also the calming of her concern convinced that imitation was flattery. So Paola and Carlo might have their *celebrazione*, some sacred applause, even the appreciation of voices and a thousand and more *trombe*."

"I could hear them." Donatella grasped his arm.

"No time to lose." He took off his jacket and pushed up his sleeves, tapping the table, at least composing a strategy. "There's still the wedding. A performance like *vino perfetto*, not too heavy or light, neither sharp nor sweet. Like a fine lady."

"I can help you chose the music."

"Despite the accusing eyes of *Genova*?"

She looked, as he did, towards the back of the house, up to the second floor and the face in the window.

"*Domani*?"

"Yes." She really didn't want to seem that eager. "What time?"

"I have a lesson late morning, followed by an assignation."

"So you'll return by three?"

"No, not before four. I've narrowed it down to half a dozen possibilities. Shall we include *Nònna*?"

Donatella felt disappointment she knew she shouldn't. "That would certainly please her."

"As I thought I was born too late to. *Così*, off to bed," he forgot his coat, halfway down the garden steps, a little less dismissive as she caught up to him with it, "like good children."

The next afternoon, waiting for Signor Stradella reminded her grandmother of other *compositori* who were better lovers than friends, poets than practitioners, more certain of leaving than arriving. Nonna didn't give up on him, even as too many churches tolled five and the next half hour, refusing supper until he returned. Donatella was more patient for his apology, an afterthought to his dash into the room and flash of teeth, toss of his coat over the reading chair, loosening of the lace on his sleeves and silk around his neck. Although he was late, he hadn't forgotten, especially not the music, spreading it out at Nonna's feet.

CHAPTER EIGHT

It was hard to choose. Should they suspect or enjoy him, the expensive scent of his afternoon implying an evening rendezvous, as well? He straddled the vanity stool pulled to the bed, leaning towards Nonna, who slapped his hand. "You handle your compositions like afterthoughts," she said, shuffling pages across the covers, "when they're the reason you're here."

"No other?"

"In my time *cantanti* were often treated like acrobats of the throat instead of *artisti* of the heart."

"Ah, *signora*."

"I had hoped you wouldn't do that."

"Sometimes they don't have a heart."

"Or you mistake what they don't give you because of what they do."

He saw what had made Nonna fascinating but overly challenging. She held a page of music and began to sing.

"*Bravo*!" He stroked her cheeks, kissing her mouth.

Donatella looked away but sensed and then heard her grandmother's attention shift to her, "I know what I like to sing, but also that Donatella has an opinion."

"Only about the *musica*?"

There was no knowing if he regretted or appreciated Donatella's diplomatic lack of a reply.

"I wish I could be there." Nonna pushed up in bed so the blankets fell to reveal more than her yellowed nightgown.

Donatella brushed the back of him to cover her up, Despina suddenly in the room.

"*Signorina*, we need your verdict."

Was there anything Signor Stradella couldn't talk himself out of, a mistake he wouldn't make right, a hand not warmer in his?

"Oh, signor," Despina looked flushed, "I'm not musical."

"Be careful. He might convince you yet." Golone came into the room.

"My man. Do I have an engagement this evening?"

"Only of your choosing."

"Sì." Signor Stradella looked at Donatella and Nonna waiting for him to escape. "There is that other world."

"So different from this one?" Despina still stood close to him.

"Like the sea from the shore."

"Or a lady from a whore," Golone couldn't resist.

Her aunt didn't quite ignore him. "So, signor, as usual you dine elsewhere?"

"Well, in case," Golone realized what he had gotten away with, "I've laid out your clothes."

"As you will my corpse one day," Signor Stradella added.

***

6 luglio. Donatella's birthday was the same day as the Spinola Brignole wedding. One was worth a fuss, the other beyond counting on. Her copying was improving, evening the time to disappear as she finally accepted the help of a west facing window. Its tenant was there in spirit only, discretion the key, her aunt none the wiser, while Nubesta was easier and easier to bargain with, stealing up where, after a certain hour, she hadn't any business, waiting for trouble as Donatella meant to avoid it. Signor Stradella rarely returned before ten; with the window open, she would hear his whistle and quickly cap the ink, clean her pen, straightening the originals and copies with the freshest on top. At worst, she would meet him on the stairs, her cheeks warm and his smile weary.

In the meantime, she had a few unbelievable hours in a room with a view of the lowering sun. There were things she might find in any other, including a dark June hearth, cluttered tables and empty chairs, rugs with curled corners, curtains catching the breath of windows, and candles dripping like icing down their holders. But where else could she be involved with genius, cradle a lute and stroke a harpsichord whose hinged lift exposed its inner workings, half finished masterpieces on its lyre-shaped mind? Back at the table quill and cigar stubs told of more time than she spent there and of a bolder ambition approved and disapproved for the same reason, supported by coffee as much as patrons, but especially by the insistence of something greater yet.

The music inspired by myth and muse was appreciated for the magnificence of a smile, too. So she wondered where it went and who else it touched, feeling she should care, less and less inhibited by some personal involvement as long as he didn't know she was.

***

In her ignorance, Despina decided an invitation to the rehearsal at *Santa Maria Maddalena* included her. Donatella sat stiffly beside her, hardly hearing anything over her resentment—and not just of her aunt. She should have expected Signor Stradella's attention to the skillful and slender soprano, the performance needing her devotion even if his heart did not.

Donatella couldn't help consider what beauty and talent would have done for her. Was there ever a time when she might have become what she was meant to, distinct and determined, love neither making nor breaking her, a brush or pen or both revealing and remembering her longer?

"It's not too late," Signor Stradella had stopped the music, leaning out of the gallery, "to make changes."

"Who are they?" the singer asked.

"The *pubblico*, my sweet bird."

"I hope they have better taste in music than dress."

"They're *signorine modeste*," he chided her more than defended anyone.

"Then how do you know them?" the bass questioned what the girl wouldn't.

Signor Stradella rarely hesitated, whether to speak or act, but as Despina rose indignantly he was silent longer than she could wait or allow Donatella to, either.

"Shall we say the hand of *destino*?"

Donatella wouldn't agree, and he didn't seem disappointed, turning to the beauty beside but not for him.

"My forgetful bird, can we try to get this right?"

Nonna thought Donatella was a fool every time she denied what was in her heart. Then her grandmother had a performer's need for melodrama, so who knew what the truth was or cared when her voice reached such heights and her eyes were so enchanting?

"Donatella," Despina hadn't left without her, "are you coming?"

"*Signorina,*" Signor Stradella created an ugly sound with his bow and voice, "Leave. Or *silenzio*!"

The soprano took a step back and the bass clapped his hands. A lutenist looked up, as he almost never did, the *violone da gamba* suddenly not large enough for its master to hide behind. Donatella quickly tightened her skirt into the pew as voices lifted above a *continuo* that might go on forever. She found herself praying; not like during mass, in repetition and humility, but with inspired—even courageous—feeling for the life she was given, its beautiful beginning and every anticipation, pause and revision, clarity and confusion, single voice and sudden harmonies, discord nothing more than an untuned string or slowly turned page.

"We need you up here," Signor Stradella called to her.

"I know it by heart," the young singer challenged his motive.

"Let me hear it so."

"But," she finally acknowledged the instrumentalists, "they must follow me."

"It isn't a *parata.*"

She did what Donatella never could, trembling and weeping and falling against him such that the mumblings of the old women in the chapel at the end of the aisle weren't about the Holy Mother. He was at once sorry, wiping her cheeks and holding her hand.

Donatella claimed she didn't go to another rehearsal because it was overly warm in the church at a time when she was inclined to headaches. Signor Stradella said he understood—more likely the reason she wouldn't speak of.

She didn't want him to think she had lost interest.

"How did it go today?"

"The *parata* will be ready."

"Your soprano has a nice voice."

"Ah, *signorina,*" he greeted her aunt, who had been making the most of his apology.

It had come quickly, the day of Despina's humiliation, Signor Stradella finding her reading in the worst light, leaning over her until she was showing him her book and laughing with the usual conceit.

Donatella didn't think he knew she had been eavesdropping.

A few days later he needed to speak with Despina again, this time requiring Donatella to stand outside her salon.

Whatever he was up to took longer than an apology.

"She's agreed."

"To what?"

"My plan for you."

"To continue copying?"

"She doesn't know of that."

"Oh. What else?"

"A wedding."

Donatella realized what he meant, surprised by what she had first thought of.

"You'll wear the sky. And do something different with your hair." He arranged the air around her head. "With red, no, yellow flowers. You need *luminosità*, not fire."

He was truly composing her, coming very close to resting his hand on her chest. "And a bunch here, too, with a spray of fern."

"Yes." Her aunt might have noticed. "It could be beneficial if you're seen in society. Still you must not appear too high."

Signor Stradella hardly begged to differ. "She'll be looking down on them all."

Nonna also gave Donatella tips: "All *musicisti* would rather do it their way, all *virtuosi*. But at the moment of performance they are a river flowing in one direction," she smiled as she thought of something, "with a splash here and there."

On her thirty-sixth birthday Donatella wore blue linen, yellow jasmine, and feathery green for the marriage of nobility to nobility. Signor Stradella stood behind the rising soprano, involved with the lute and gamba parts even as he played the violin. Donatella was squeezed into the shadows, smelling the resin on his bow and musk on his collar, reminding herself she was in church but not convinced by hands and voices weaving prayers as light and material as the lace on their sleeves and necks, or even by the mass that took forever to acknowledge the joy of the occasion with the shame of what it allowed.

The music was its only redemption; strange that it should go so unrecognized.

"But, my *angelo,*" Signor said to the soprano missing applause, "such prestige is ours."

"And a few *scudi,* too." The bass held out a hand Signor Stradella slapped.

"You'll engage me at the theater?" the girl persisted.

"If you can engage me there."

"Oh, I forgot." She petted his arm. "Why were you dismissed?"

"Rumor has it," the bass sought playful revenge, "he enjoyed his position too much."

"Rumors can amuse," Signor Stradella sounded annoyed, the gamba player offering a sympathetic chord, "as long as they don't accuse."

"Maestro," called a commanding voice from below.

"Ah. *Signore Spinola.*"

"Encore," the gray wig and elaborately cuffed arms meant to conduct him, "for the happy couple."

Signor Stradella beckoned Donatella into the light, until she was closer to him than anyone else, unpinning the nosegay from her dress and planting it with a whisper behind her ear. "And a happier day for who was born."

"Maestro," Signor Spinola wouldn't be ignored, "will you play again?"

Signor Stradella stiffened, yet still sounded obliging, "*Naturalmente, signore.* We're not finished yet."

PART THREE

THE OBJECTION

CHAPTER NINE

The complaints were anonymous. Alessandro and Lonati laughed over crimes committed for camaraderie, drinking the day away, or so it seemed when Golone stumbled downstairs with another empty bottle.

"Listen." Donatella wasn't the only one under the spell of their playing.

The two maestros were unlikely friends except as their restlessness and violins bonded and misbehaved. Like another associated with them—the *Romano*—who touched ladies' faces while fixing their hair, Alessandro could hardly avoid beauty letting down its guard to beauty. The only advantage a hunchback might claim was if sympathy had its way. Despina was outraged that it was almost the end of August before she heard the gossip from June. Some letters demanded exile, others offering the means for roguishness and genius to become more established.

"I always resist what isn't offered," Alessandro confessed.

Lonati's face lifted "Spoken like a man who's never wanting."

The shame of Genoa was its longing to be shameful. A gentleman's ordinary gesture revealed a diamonded watch for the telling of wealth, curls in a wig and ribbons on sleeves showing vanity, gleaming buttons self-important. Despite her long black cloak, a lady revealed a pink shoe as she stepped down from a carriage, two servants one more than should be attending to her publically. Theatrics and other entertainments were hidden in places easily found, music outside church or ceremony unnecessary except for idle enjoyment.

"When asked to stay in *Genova,*" Alessandro was overly serious, "there wasn't anything I was obliged to do. How could I know its finest *signorine* and *signore* would be so interested in singing?"

Lonati eyed Despina, not sure she was spy or sympathizer. "And so this city and its females should be grateful for your generosity."

"And mine." Until then Despina had grumbled to everyone else that nothing was offered for Lonati staying longer than it should have taken him to find new lodgings. There was some compensation in Alessandro's willingness to share him for meetings on the stairs, *bavareisa* in the breakfast room, cards, and even gambling before suppers on the terrace.

"Of course I know what to expect from musicians." Despina meant to disturb them, unlike Donatella finishing the evening's watering. "That's why Signor Garibaldi chose this house."

"For one of us only," Alessandro informed his hunchbacked acquaintance.

Lonati was more uncomfortable than his abnormality forced him to be, getting up to stretch. Despina immediately took his seat.

Alessandro didn't look at her. "You might've done better to stay in *Milano*, Carlo."

"And miss the Genoese gossip?"

"Miss making it."

"And let you have all the fun?"

"Is that what I'm having?"

"The barrel is almost empty." Donatella demonstrated the lightness of her watering can.

Alessandro leaned back, not relaxed. "The sun sets for heat, not rain."

"That is good, isn't it?"

"In *Dicembre*."

"Not for Saturday?"

"Perhaps it would be better to call off the cloak and dagger."

Lonati nearly fell on him. "They'll love it as impossibly as they do you!"

Golone passed Donatella coming up the stone steps, presenting a silver platter of parsley dressed oysters.

Alessandro rose when Despina did. "You won't stay?"

"No. Shellfish doesn't agree with me."

"A woman of *Liguria?*"

"I've never liked the sea. Or anything that comes from it."

He glanced at Donatella, who had heard it all before. She filled the awkwardness with picking a lemon from one of the potted trees.

"Will you also add the flavor of your *società*?" He reached for a small knife stabbed into an oyster.

Donatella reservedly accepted it with his smooth talk. Alessandro sat while she dissected and squeezed the overripe fruit, Lonati beside him again, Golone standing nearby with folded arms and a sinister smile.

Lonati grabbed and swallowed greedily while Alessandro seemed to be looking for a pearl, or perhaps just the prettiest shell, suddenly slapping an insatiable hand.

"What's the matter?" Lonati finally wiped his mouth.

"You take advantage."

"Of what's offered." He expected imitation to flatter, or at least amuse.

Alessandro was almost ugly. "*Parassita.* You're crooked like a miser with someone else's money."

Lonati turned to Donatella, if only to give time for Alessandro's apology.

"Ape! Go find a *cavèrna.*"

Donatella wanted Lonati to leave, but not like that. "He can't find somewhere else to stay tonight."

"Is that what I meant?" Alessandro used the smoothness of his voice again. "Now you can sit."

"But where is he going?"

Lonati edgily answered, "A house that welcomes deformed men."

"Not a *deformità* but *distinzione,* Carlo." Alessandro hoped that if his friend and foe heard he was listening. "Follow him, Golone."

"What about you?"

"I'm staying home tonight."

"I see." Golone squinted at Donatella.

"You don't. Go on."

"A night off?"

"It's all yours."

Golone had no further objection as he left. "And yours."

"He's so careless."

"Golone?" Donatella could hardly follow him.

"No. *Il Gobbo.*"

"You shouldn't call Signor Lonati that."

"Everyone does."

"It offends him."

"*Bène,* it also serves him."

"Now he feels unwelcome here."

"As I may," Alessandro was brilliantly mannered again, "if you don't sit." He peeled her hands off the back of the chair, placed her in it, tilting an oyster to her lips. "You're not like your aunt, I hope?"

Her answer was obvious, drooling down her chin, his finger catching and putting it to his lips.

"You must tell me about your journey from the sea."

"I'd have to make most of it up."

"*Allora,* there's an *opera* in it."

"The theater is much more fantastic than life."

"Except for those who invent it." He waved his hand over the platter. "*Qui.* Let's not waste the life ... or death ... of the *ostrica.*" His mouth quickly sucked in the last. "I may just go too far."

She hoped he was talking about Lonati.

"I'm sure he'll find some *consolazione.*"

"You've been friends a long time."

"How do you know?"

"He told me."

"*Così,* you speak to him more than me?"

If ever they'd been rivals, certainly not over her. "The afternoon he arrived."

"*Sì.* To beg more than your pardon."

Nubesta saw the visitor first, made the sign of the cross and ran back to the kitchen. Donatella answered the door left open. The man there was stooped with baggage at his feet. She asked who he was. *A collaborator.* She didn't understand until he held up his violin easier than his head. *Carlo Ambrogio Lonati.* She assumed he was looking for Alessandro. He strained his neck to show the spark in his eyes. *Weren't you?*

"He was all ears," Alessandro drank from a glass with little to offer, "when I mentioned your hospitality."

"You're the reason he came."

"Such *diplomazia.*" Without wine for comfort, Alessandro loosened his collar. "But you fed him?"

"In the breakfast room. He was glad of an early lunch of bread and soup which I brought him in case Nubesta offered insults."

"And welcomed him to wait?"

"He was hungry but also glad of a sofa."

"No longer or shorter than the stretch of his legs."

"He was glad to sit down."

"Then you asked him to stay? Ah. You implied he could."

"Not until he told me that on returning from Milan he'd discovered his apartment was no longer available."

"Did he tell you the reason?"

She hesitated, but thought she might learn more than she could tell, "Only that you knew why."

Alessandro got up and pulled his shirt over his trousers, walking to the end of the terrace where a brittle holly was meant for cooler situations. Donatella's father never doubted its survival. Like Alessandro, he was always challenging and impossible, planting a foreign bush and leaving it to do what it could where it was. Alessandro returned to the table and leaned over, his hair falling onto her face, too, offering the first relief of the evening. "Only why it has nothing to do with me."

Nubesta and lantern bounced up to the terrace, Alessandro's smile welcoming both, the girl soon close enough to push her body against him.

"Clean up and come in," Despina demanded, although only while she was watching from the conservatory door, Nubesta making the most of Alessandro looking down on her.

"Go along, *innamorato*. Or we'll be on the streets like Lonati."

"I'll get those." Donatella embraced numerous empty bottles. "You won't really turn the poor man out?"

"Poor man?" Alessandro swayed like Nubesta but for a different reason. "*Il Gobbo della Regina*? Of nobly defected birth? Partner in *crimine*? And *contrapunto*? And *opera buffa*?"

Lonati had similarly described their association, playing in *Roma, Venezia*, and now at its most critical in *Genova*. Once in the front hallway, Donatella was convinced Alessandro didn't mean anything he said.

"Golone! Where is he?"

"You sent him away."

"I need more *vino*."

"You don't." As Donatella helped him upstairs her aunt's discomfort was an antidote to her own.

"Then more copies."

"For Saturday?"
"And *posterità*."

CHAPTER TEN

A carriage was waiting. Awkwardly handling skirts and guilt out of the house, there wasn't time for Donatella to hesitate with wondering where it might take her or how high the step up.

When she was twelve an open vehicle was still acceptable, the smell of horses and leather mingling with jasmine water and nauseating in the heat. She remembered that its first movement was abrupt so she fell forward and back again, her hands and knees assailants, apologies lost in laughter. Except her aunt wasn't amused and kept pushing the curls off her face. Her mother's tightly gloved hand around hers was some reassurance they weren't headed for more trouble than her grandmother knew how to handle. Nonna had the talent for attracting an invitation beyond the walls of the city and their demoralized situation, although Aunt Despina insisted it was extended because she gave respectability to the family.

Leaving home still made Donatella feel insecure, not special.

"*Signorina*, may I ride with you?"

This time the carriage was smaller and enclosed.

"I'm riding with you."

Alessandro shouted out as he climbed in, "You haven't forgotten anything?"

"Especially not how I hate horses," Golone answered, their transport on loan without a proper driver.

Alessandro's knees nudged Donatella's as he sat opposite. "Did he see you get in?"

"No."

"*Buon. Finalmente* I take you away." His head went out the window. "What are we waiting for?"

"Will we pick up the hunchback?" Golone thought Alessandro was the only passenger where his instrument and music left room for two.

"From where?"

"The Roman's?"

"No."

The journey began and Donatella lunged into Alessandro's lap.

He respectfully helped her resume her place. "I prefer to walk. It improves the health."

She didn't want to remind him that *Santa Maria Maddalena,* books, windows, and a small garden were the extent of her travels. She didn't have to.

"But, daughter of a *marinaio,* you should've ridden the waves."

In a sharp turn passengers and cargo slid and squeezed left then right, Alessandro quickly responding to keep his violin from falling off the seat, Donatella making several attempts to gather up the music that had slid to the floor.

"*Bène* you're riding them now, in a *monsone*!"

The carriage jolted to a stop, Golone yelling something Donatella didn't hear.

"Will you get us arrested?"

Golone's swearing continued even as the carriage began to move again, Alessandro reaching out to cover her ears.

Even as a young girl she had wondered how she could live so long in one place, excited by escape, following the bay opening and closing with merchant docks and ships, none of which offered her father's seared cheeks, English-brown eyes, and boyish wave. Her mother didn't face that disappointment, her head thrown back, ignoring the comments of her older sister. Donatella might have been a hostage of their differences if Nonna hadn't captured her imagination instead.

"Does it feel like an *avventura*?"

She didn't suspect Alessandro's motives as much as his manners. "I can't believe I got away. Not even Nubesta saw me leave." She fidgeted and held the thick leather folder higher, her arms around it. "I should have let Nonna know."

"I did. She promised to tell your aunt."

"No."

"She'll worry about you."

"About how it looks."

"I was thinking of my reputation also."

The carriage quickened to go less slowly uphill. They both leaned towards a small view of the full bay, their cheeks close to touching, Donatella putting opportunity over modesty with a sigh.

"We're almost there. I heard this isn't your first visit to the *villa* at *Fasolo*."

"I was a child."

"You're still wide-eyed." He pulled back. "But relax, we won't be judged as ourselves."

They arrived, their carriage last in a line on the *via San Benedetto*, the rise of statues and designed woods shadowing the north façade of the palace through a protruding portal of columns crowned with the Doria coat of arms.

"No wonder Lonati was left out."

When Golone discovered Donatella, he ignored her struggle with dress and descent, Alessandro impatient to hand him his violin. She hoped they would be early or late to avoid scrutiny, but they were on time for her to be judged as an unescorted woman passing through a hall made for giants, past tapestries and frescoed thunderbolts and up a staircase of even grander portraits, Alessandro having been intercepted by the gentlemen of ladies who knew him less discreetly than he did them.

Out of fashion herself, Donatella didn't watch for the trailing of skirts until she stumbled.

"You have it!" An unknown lady was eying the music Donatella was responsible for. "Sandro told me to find you."

"He did?"

"Well, a woman in forget-me-not blue looking like she knows better."

The silken seductress lifted her bare shoulders, the pearl and emerald decoration of her neck more revealing. "I need to prepare."

"You'll sing today?"

"I hope so. I was quite hoarse this morning."

"Summer colds are the worst."

"No, it's nerves." The stranger bowed her head, cinnamon curls dangling like catkins. "I've only been heard in lessons. Other than by Sandro, just family."

"Our comfort or captors."

"Oh," the woman's flounces and ribbons adorned Donatella too, "you're so right. My brothers would prefer I never speak, let alone sing, although they mean well and my husband humors me."

"With Signor Stradella?"

The lady's smile was as ready as her answer, "The door is always open, others just beyond."

"No one objects to you performing today?"

"They won't know until I do."

Similar strategies weren't all they had in common. "The reason you worry."

"Not really." The other woman was highly motivated in view of something—or someone, Alessandro walking by as though he didn't notice.

***

She remembered the aviary, stretching Cypresses and thick myrtles caging it against the west walls of the palace, containing but not restricting colorful movements and songs, iron and netting holding its residents to a contract of protection for appearances. Pheasants were the principals, strutting and shimmering around fountains and flapping up to swaying perches, their voices more imposing than entertaining. This was the one attraction her mother and aunt agreed upon, lifting the little girl between them; she immediately noticed that ordinary birds intermingled with the elite of their own kind.

It was still a trap, no matter its illuminating scenery and cupola climaxing in a motionless eagle. Donatella moved through sun lined arcades, perspiring, the leather folder against her chest which had tightened like her shoes.

"So this is where you'll sing." Donatella meant to be alarming, pointing out the main terrace where the arrangement of chairs, music stands, and spraying bouquets wasn't settled yet.

"I can't do it!"

"You can," Donatella said unwillingly.

She sank onto a bench that hadn't been there all those years ago, untying and flipping through the music on her lap, pheasants flapping down from their noon roost as sprawling bushes shook with their cellmates' opinions. The wire mesh behind the bars had been replaced and must have been stronger, no sign of commoners within its bounds now.

It wasn't a great but indulged voice practicing scales and a piece of aria, not even moving the jewels around its owner's neck and piercing her ears. Nonna would have identified her as a *dilettante* who never sang for her life.

"Oh, I always get this passage wrong," her clammy hands did some damage, "and even spoiled the beautiful copy, your hard work."

Donatella wasn't sure she should agree.

"I hope you'll forgive me. Sandro will be annoyed."

"Not if I fix it before he sees."

"No wonder he uses you." The other woman walked into the heat of the day, a piece of the music against her heart.

"Signora!"

Donatella wasn't the first to catch up to her.

"Signora, you shouldn't be on your own," insisted a middle-aged lady of less breeding than elegance. "What's that?"

"Music."

"Why do you have it?"

"For my debut."

"What do you mean?"

"What do you think all those singing lessons were for?"

"To stop your pouting."

"Promise not to tell. Everyone will know soon enough."

"I won't let you do it."

"What harm can it do? Ask Signor Stradella's woman. Don't look so shocked. I don't know what else to call her."

Donatella finally introduced herself.

"Well, little Donata, I'm Maria Caterina."

"To be addressed as Signora Garibaldi." the chaperone corrected, too late to stop her mistress from encouraging more inappropriate behavior, waving to where Alessandro had climbed.

Mother didn't mind, but Aunt Despina was appalled as a young Donatella skipped in and out of the crisscrossing loggias separating a prince's paradise from Neptune's. She was soon on the bridge and crest of a wave, feeling the freedom, the sun setting her course, vying for notice if not all it attracted. So the wind went out of her sails and she was anchored and back on land, preferring a scolding to attention that didn't care who she wanted to be.

Now in her place was a flowing cream and gold figure, like a decoratively delicious *torta* lifted onto a pedestal. His breezy wig, shiny face, stiff cuffs, and jeweled hands conducted the construction of an opera with more frustration than fraternity.

"He needs the music now." Donatella remembered a promise as she broke it. "I don't suppose it matters if you hold on to yours."

"You're being foolish again, Maria." The chaperone meant Donatella to be ignored.

"Do you think I am?" the beautiful woman asked anyway.

Donatella was also surprised she had an answer, "I think you must be."

CHAPTER ELEVEN

The stage was set. Alessandro was calmer coming down from his critical viewpoint, even congratulating Lonati who had found his own way there from wherever he had spent the last few days and nights. They kissed cheeks and joked with each other, Alessandro directing Golone to add a scrolled-back chair to the semicircle where other suffering musicians hadn't expected a Queen's hunchback to be relegated either.

"Ah! The *stelle* have come out in the middle of the day!" Alessandro finally greeted the sopranos not immediately forgiving his neglect.

Donatella knew one was Margherita of Bologna, the other a great relief.

"You see, my sister has come after all."

Alessandro clapped his hands and looked over his shoulder. "To save us from a *situazione.*"

The two confidently plump ladies didn't care to understand him or for the heat, the one about to become *Doriclea* wondering what was wrong with opera in the shade.

"It's already shadowed in controversy."

"As every performance should be." Lonati strayed from his place, lifting the sister's hand in an effort without reward.

"*Cara signora,* you still know the part?" Alessandro rescued and endangered her at the same time.

"As I do my own mind," she stepped closer to his concern, petting his arm, "which isn't so small. Let me look it over."

"*Naturalmente.*" He reached out to Donatella who had been following his movements. "The *musica* for *Lucinda.*"

"But ... you need two sopranos."

"*Sì.* Here are the best."

"But what about Signora Garibaldi?"

His not hearing was so no one else did; he took the folder and searched it.

"It's not there," she confessed as he found out.

Lonati's laugh was as warped as his back. Alessandro didn't consider it funny, too many singers and little time before a gossip-hungry audience swarmed out of the palace's cloisters and side gardens.

"You must get it." Alessandro was only professionally desperate.

***

Signora Garibaldi finally took her seat, watched mercilessly like the finely dressed birds in the aviary, although she couldn't flap her wings let alone sing her song. She was only steps away from disgracing herself when Donatella persuaded her to give up the copy crumpled at the edges from anxiety about performing and then not performing. Maria Caterina had nothing to say except with eyes grayer in tears.

"Maestro, come here," the second soprano squealed. "Look at the state of this. Especially these blotches."

"Ah. It should've been powdered more." Even Alessandro's apology sought Donatella's assistance.

"And you should stick to ladies who don't cry." Lonati tuned his violin.

The performers, even the sopranos, were as relaxed and ready as Alessandro wasn't. He checked the players' positioning, music on stands, pitch of each instrument including his violin, and the angle of the sun. Donatella answered the sisters' demands for refreshment from the jug and glasses concealed behind a heart-shaped flower display; they drank without gratitude or for her pulling out their skirts and patting their necks before Alessandro testily directed them to their places.

Donatella retreated with Golone to the wings of the western arches where he revealed the flask he had brought along for thirsty boredom, toasting her as just another servant to the temperament of divas and masters.

Perhaps it was at that moment she surrendered to the possibility of a new fate, one that would neither leave her indifferent nor waiting for something better. Everything depended on Alessandro fulfilling his calling to center stage, bowing head and shoulders towards Prince and Princess Doria who smiled reassuringly before cordially commanding silence.

What was he waiting for? The bow raising his right sleeve, he turned his face away and lowered his chin, his own hair covering any expression of nerves. The violin bent his left arm, curling its hand, straightening his shoulders and curving his back so his hips disappeared and legs lengthened, butterfly knotted shoes closely parted like feet on a pedestal table. The slightly past midday sun was a spotlight on the terrace, his creamy coat and the crimson of Margherita's skirt. There was no breeze or any kind of movement, not even a cough or whisper.

Lonati stood and was told to sit down. Alessandro was perfectly posed for a portrait or memory or the recognition of God, raising his sight, an aspiring suitor preparing to declare his intentions.

Hands and laps held programs Donatella had duplicated for *Una Storia del Cavalieri, Il Trionfo Erroneo di Amore.* Alessandro wasn't confident the *Genovese* elite would admittedly enjoy it, unless he kept it at a distance in a self-indulged city like *Venezia,* accompanied by elaborate sets and costumes, effects, and even dancing. There hadn't been money or time for such an undertaking, so perhaps his hesitation considered how much depended on the manipulation of his music to refine and even refute the folly of its subject.

Within moments of his bow sliding into sound a trick was also triumph, holding back impulse for contemplation and swashbuckling for delicacy, putting serenity in strings before the highs and lows of singers. *Doriclea* loved *Fidalbo* not *Olindo,* and every note believed her until Alessandro played with them, Lonati following in friendly imitation, the *castrato* coming forward. Eventually the *continuo* slowed everyone, underscoring virtuosity and relieving it, too, if not for long. The principal of *obstinato* was practiced for connection and contest, a single motif tossed around in slightly different versions like a rumor or hope of one, voices and instruments in competing agreement.

Alessandro was master of entertaining and editorializing, stealing the show without taking anything from the roles of lovers and go-betweens, spoilers, and servants, giving character to romance, farce, and delusion. He stood apart from the ensemble with nods for their faithfulness, or squints and frowns for what he hadn't thought of. Less and less he was concerned with an audience irrelevant to his sense of achievement or regret, artistic isolation suiting him as much as flamboyancy.

By the intermission, Golone could barely stand. A servant from the palace brought a basket of fruit, and it seemed only Donatella wondered who would drive them home. Alessandro sucked on a plum, lost in his thoughts, even ignoring the sopranos sweeping in front of him complaining again about the heat and Lonati joking that they might cool themselves in one of the fountains.

"Was she very upset?" Alessandro acknowledged the problem Donatella had hardly resolved.

"Of course."

"I shouldn't make such promises."

"Why do you?"

"You know why." He threw the plum's pit at Golone. "You don't, do you?"

Before he lifted the violin again, Alessandro squinted into the shadows where what waited for him wasn't what he was looking for. The first act set up the second's misunderstandings, laughter, and tears, the unforgivable always a story of forgiving. Melody encouraged words that explained, cajoled, and brought the company together in relief of a happy ending and increasing shade from the palace, making the afternoon as long and short as the applause and memory of it. Alessandro held his heart and took a bow, artist and pragmatist, knowing that if the critics liked what they heard they might forget what was said. His celebrity was like the heat of summer, longed for and grumbled about. At the end, his hand extended to the prince, more slowly to the princess, who chided him for such formality with a stretch and kiss on his cheek.

An announcement was made for everyone to take their appetites to the *Loggia dei Eroi.*

"Only after everyone else," Golone loudly advised.

"We'll see about that." Margherita took her sister's arm and a chance that nothing would stop them.

"Well, gentlemen," Lonati addressed his fellow accompanists, "shall the ladies prove us cowards?"

"It's what they do best," Alessandro murmured sulkily.

"Ah, the dragon will be waiting for her return," Golone noted another reason for Donatella's frowning.

"Why?" Lonati was vaguely interested.

"Reputations," Golone kissed the top of his master's hand helping him up.

"Or *gelosia,"* Alessandro knew what he was saying.

As did Lonati. "Jealous of what? Her niece wasting time with you?"

Donatella was placated with a stroke on the blistering bareness of her arm, the elegance of buttons on an open lapel, a diamond studding the loosened knot of a cravat, slightly silvered hair and shadow on a chin up to the glisten of bristled lips.

"So we've waited long enough?" Lonati challenged. "Golone, not you. Put the instruments in the shade and guard them."

"Ah, *il Gobbo* doesn't have his own man," Alessandro pulled her against him, "so orders mine."

"Genoa hasn't been so appreciative of me."

"For you act the servant yourself."

"Please don't," Donatella whined.

"What do you plead for?"

"You're making a spectacle."

"And we thought the performance was over." Lonati was laughing at her.

Alessandro leaned over to him. "She can only deny us a smile."

"Something you might value?" Lonati was surprising, thinking so much of her.

Alessandro waved a hand and then again to one of the violists. "Are you hungry?" he asked him.

"Always."

"*Così*," Alessandro gave him the folder, "let *musica* be the food."

"Not of love." Maria Caterina stepped onto the stage at last.

Alessandro couldn't resist her. "This is not wise."

"You're cruel." Her fan almost touched his lips.

"I'm forced to be."

"By your ambitions?"

"And yours."

The incidental music of viols and lutes or just the sparkle of Maria Caterina's eyes and necklace convinced Alessandro to walk away with her, so anyone might see but not know where they had gone if, like Donatella, they didn't care to. She disappeared, too, clumsy around emptied chairs through the narrow passageway under the terraced wall behind them, further than the control of the palace stretched. There the sun reigned in colorful and aromatic compartments, low, escapable, and penetrable myrtle fortresses holding daisies, carnations, and rosemary to the vague memory of a design. Fountains east and west were ignored for Neptune's height and scepter. How could she not be attracted to a sea god on land even if he was going nowhere, forever riding on legless horses and the motionless winds and spraying breath of gryphons? He was a central figure surrounded by myth, sculpted benches, and terracotta pots cracked by constricted roots; flares and spikes, creeping sedums and thyme making a circle of friends that did and didn't complement him.

Donatella ascended to the balcony of the redundant sea *loggia* and was caught on the wheel of admiring Neptune, gripping its northern railing, leaning over perilously. She felt ill in the heat of spinning around and around with the shapes and shapelessness of the palatial park on an axle of imagination, faster and faster, blurring the lines of sight and what could be her downfall.

"*Qui.* I've got you."

She struggled against the warmth of Alessandro's chest.

"Your fan?"

"I don't have one."

"I wondered where you'd gone."

"I thought nearer the sea."

He pointed out the public road below between princely power and the doges' reaction to it. "There's no longer a way from here."

Before she was born the wall had gone up. "From anywhere."

"Ah. That *opera.* Yet to be written."

"In opera something happens."

"Like this?" His arm went around her waist.

CHAPTER TWELVE

She couldn't object. It was even more dizzying down the ramp and across the white-hot gravel to reach Neptune's sphere, Alessandro splashing water on his face. He had left his jacket on one of the benches, throwing it over a shoulder to support her with the other more reservedly than before.

"Are we leaving now?"

"I can't return you sick."

"I feel better." She was cooler under the pergola arching along the west side of the formal garden, shaded by heavy wisteria vines with yellowing leaves and velvety seedpods. "How wonderful it must be in spring."

"If the clouds are rainless," he looked up and ahead, "a better time for *opera* in the open air."

"Yes."

"The one you'll help me write."

They passed by a few chances for sitting intimately under the ironwork passageway leading them, slower and slower, back to the palace.

"Is this all right?"

She didn't disagree with his suggestion for resting where the aviary could be heard.

"The *prima scena* will be on a ship."

"It will?"

"No. In a bed chamber."

"Oh."

"The heroine gazing into a mirror," he wrote behind his eyes, "and what she's missing."

"How do you know where to start?"

"Where it finishes."

"Happily, of course."

"You tell me."

"If she doesn't mind being alone—"

"Ah." He was ready for the challenge. "As chosen or happens?"

"Perhaps there's no difference."

"*Opera* is not about philosophy."

"Then the romantic?"

"*Sì.*" He wasn't ready to commit himself. "But mostly recompense."

"Creative fulfillment."

"*Ancora.* Philosophy."

"I know. You have to make a living."

"*Bène,* I might've been a priest. You smile."

"Did you consider it?"

"My mother thought I was too handsome."

"Seriously."

"*Seriamente.* Step-uncles proved it wasn't for me. One died by the sword, the other lived a different bodily death." He patted her knee. "At least I'm reverent in *motetti* and *liturgie.* Where were we?"

"Recompense," she pronounced as though she had never said it before.

"Ah, *sì.*" He clapped. "So little and so much. A lazy servant and comfortable apartment, a few *doubloons,* a chance to settle down, to work or not, and kindnesses, many kindnesses."

"You're a rich man."

"*Così.*" He was determined to woo her imagination. "She looks through her dresses."

"You mean, in the opera?"

"At the loveliest, the lowest cut."

The ones Donatella thought she would never wear again. Yet here he was tracing the neckline that once held the expectation of youth if not beauty, finally only attracting an illustrative touch.

"Though she doesn't believe they will make any difference."

"She knows they won't."

"Ah. Beauty isn't a rule but *impressione.* And so we bring in the tall, confident *tenore*—except as he's afraid to admit his *sentimento,* standing in the background. The staging is *importante:* a platform against a stormy sky, with a rocking motif by the skip of a fourth in the *basso.*"

"It could be her father."

"It isn't."

"Or a ghost."

"That's better." He huddled up to her. "Tell me. And I'll disguise it in *mitologia*."

She tried to speak, if just to breathe.

He gave her some space. "You're still unwell." He stood, helped her up, and they were walking together, then apart. "Ah, Golone, am I missed?"

"Not by me. The princess."

Alessandro stepped towards him so Donatella knew she shouldn't listen to what he said, "And *Signora Garibaldi*?"

"Gone. And soon forgotten."

"Like a dream."

"I thought you hadn't slept with her."

***

The *Salone dei Giganti* had emptied for the princess to dance across the large shiny floor like a peasant with her young son. The gamba player stopped and stood, bowing to Alessandro, who encouraged him to continue. The princess only half-twirled, sending the boy into Alessandro's arms, giving Donatella the chance to wait where she might go unnoticed.

"At last." The princess welcomed Alessandro as informally with her hand. "Have you eaten?" She took the child from him, whispering something into the boy's ear. When she put him down he ran out of the room. "I did not see you on the terrace."

"No. My hunger was interrupted."

The gamba player laughed. The princess didn't.

"Because of too much sun."

"Oh." Princess Doria was reassured and still concerned. "Do you need a doctor?" She snapped her fingers for the stiff attendant at the doors beyond a white marble fireplace, Donatella glad its only flames were in the medallion of *Prometheus* on a black stoned canopy.

"A drink. Not *vino*."

"Of course," she made sure her servant heard. "Water, with a little lemon, not too cold. And some *biscotti* and soft cheese. In the Zodiac room, the windows opened."

"Thank you." Donatella stayed at a distance.

"Who is this?" the princess sounded hopeful.

Alessandro brought Donatella forward. "*Signorina Cavanna* Hanley."

Donatella curtsied, wondering how he knew so much about her.

"English?"

"My father."

"Her grandmother was a fine *soprano.*"

"And you sing, too?"

"Not to be heard."

"She copies," Alessandro put it another way.

"Not you, I hope."

"With a constant hand."

"She might give to you?"

"I wouldn't deny it."

"Perfect. Now, before she faints—Sandro! If you are really concerned—"

Their arms hooked behind Donatella, conniving her abduction to another room on the same floor where dark woodwork, northern light and breezes were relieving. She also didn't resist a drink of lemonade or the princess ushering her to a bed behind gold striped drapes, just the loosening of her back lacing.

"Of course." The princess took the glass. "Your modesty is ours. Rest as long as you like."

"Ah, Anna Pamphilj, always *generoso*."

Neither of them left then nor while Donatella was supposed to be asleep, talking as was and wasn't expected about the music of the day and long past in *Roma,* a wedding about friendship as much as politics.

"Your music is all I remember of that day."

"You're happy?"

"Of course."

"How long now?"

"Ten years. And you are still a problem."

"It took too long for me to find refuge in *Genova*."

"I begged you to come. And when that did not work, prayed. Especially every time I heard of the danger you were in."

"*Esagerazione.*"

"You almost died! I still pray for you."

"Bless you."

"But what will keep you with us? The muses stay little in this city."

For Donatella there seemed no break in the conversation, like between the last thought at night and first in the morning.

"See I am there, the archer."

"Take aim." Alessandro obliged.

"And you, too, head down, ready to charge."

"Despite the horns, I'm a lamb."

So the Zodiac room wasn't a dream. But Donatella's listening was more effort, like seeing through a fog.

"She is not young, or as pretty as some, but available," the princess seemed to be talking to herself. "It would not be inappropriate."

"I think it might." Alessandro was still there.

"You like her? So not for that. It hardly matters."

"Where's Anna the *romantica?*"

"Rarely seen since a wedding lament."

"*Così*, you want me to write one for myself?"

"At least seem to work on it. I do not think she will mind."

Donatella sat and spoke up, "We should go."

"She wakes. But did she sleep?" Alessandro sang and suspected.

"I shouldn't be here." Donatella felt strange sliding out of bed in view of anyone, although it was only her shoes she had taken off.

"Is a palace not a fit place with fit company?"

Alessandro put his hand up. "Her aunt doesn't approve of her association with me."

Princess Doria hugged his arm and then stood as though it never happened. "Well, I must insist she does."

Donatella almost forgot what she might not thank her for.

"I will write a letter you can deliver. I will say that I was delighted you came with Maestro Stradella, and are my new hope for saving him."

In possession of the envelope with a still-warm seal, Donatella waited in the carriage for whatever was keeping Alessandro, most obviously the correctness of his goodbyes to the prince and princess. This time he sat next to her and shared the fragrance of wine and more than one woman, satisfaction of success and causing a little stir. He didn't complain about

Golone's reckless driving, drunkenness tolerant of drunkenness as insult was of injury.

"Let's continue."

"I like copying for you."

"I meant the *opera.* It isn't her papa."

"It might've been."

"No. Someone she can't resist."

There was shouting and the carriage stopped, Alessandro casually lifting over her to pass Lonati's violin through the window.

"I was almost left behind a few times." The vehicle swayed as his friendly foe stepped off the back. "But thanks for the ride."

"So this is where you're staying? *Accettabile*?"

"Better than that. I may take up hairdressing myself."

"You'd still be a crooked competitor."

"Watch him, my dear," Lonati startled her with his red face, "for he's extraordinary. Good evening!"

Donatella wanted to like Lonati. "Good evening, signor

There was ambiguity in Alessandro's voice too. "*Il Gobbo*!"

The carriage rolled forward again and Donatella was on the edge of her seat.

"What a day." Alessandro might have said it even if she wasn't there.

After the detour to drop off Lonati, they went up and down the city, silently riding the jolts and bumps and twists and turns, smelling the sea and losing the light by the time they were home, counting the bell rings and the times Golone cursed trying to convince the horses to stand still.

"*Bene, Cinderella.*" Alessandro came closer to mocking a fairytale, his kiss missing her mouth for her cheek.

PART FOUR

THE SUGGESTION

CHAPTER THIRTEEN

There was some confusion. On his way upstairs Alessandro noticed Despina coming out of her salon, glad he was alone at last and didn't always have to be, Maria Caterina near enough, a better understanding even closer.

Donatella went to her room without showing her aunt the princess' letter, for she couldn't accept its suggestion herself.

***

"Benedetto Pamphilj will be made *Cardinale.*"

The time between a kiss and word, other than in passing, had preoccupied Donatella's thoughts and almost two weeks.

"So you're off to Rome?"

"No. I'm not on that Papal list."

"Certainly."

Alessandro laughed at her tactlessness and lifted the scalloped parchment she recognized. "He's the brother of the *principessa.* There's to be a *celebrazione.*"

"She employs you, I hope."

"Certainly," he used Donatella's accent.

"And you will compose something new?"

"Dust off something old. *Alle Selve, Agli Studi.*"

"I don't know it."

"You will."

"To assist you?"

"You may be helpful. You received a summons *anche*?"

"Not from the princess." She folded the letter she had considered telling him more about.

"*Bene,* for she invites me to invite you."

Donatella wasn't under any illusions in respect to a proposal. She knew it didn't matter, despite Despina's concerns, whether she was virtuous or intended to keep so.

"Do you?"

"Only hesitating as you might want me to."

At stake was her insignificance, about to announce itself to humiliation and appear ridiculous as a contender.

"I can't refuse a princess," she answered as dutifully as Alessandro's smile didn't believe.

When the time came she showed some enthusiasm, wearing Nonna's jewelry and letting her in on the adventure.

"Shall I go without you?" Alessandro's impatience might have hoped for a different reply.

"Enjoy, my darling girl," her grandmother called out.

Alessandro was well ahead of her, music under one arm, the other swinging freely.

"Your violin?"

"I'm not playing this evening."

She almost ran to catch up with him. "Where are we going?"

"Didn't I tell you?"

Nearer than a carriage ride, farther than expected, side by side as long as she walked faster than he did. She knew how it looked, if not sure how she did squeezed into the green and bronze gown last worn for falling sonnets.

"Where's Golone?"

"To look out for us? I told him to come later." Alessandro was also unwise and unprotected in spotting velvet, drooping lace, and a dampened disarray of hair as it started to rain. "I'll be ruined." He made it seem she offered to share her cloak. The narrow alleyways were misleading, too, without direction and yet taking them where they meant to go, a sudden stop revealing their practical intimacy as another couple stepped up to the swirling gate.

"Does one get wetter running than walking?"

Whether or not Alessandro's riddle was diverting, when the door opened opinions were softened by his insistence that others enter first. Finally they went in, a busy attendant brusquely taking Donatella's cape, eager to attend to those who did not doubt their right to be there. Coughing because of candle smoke, slipping on newly waxed tiles, jostled and ignored while losing sight of her escort, she was reminded that she was unprepared for making her way in a crowded marketplace where only pomposity was for sale. The push continued up a portrait-lined turning staircase, moving slower on the landing, Alessandro pointing out the beauty of its limitations in molded stucco, gold-leaf, and overhead frescos.

"Without shame for the nudity of the *cherubini* and *frutta*."

"They look so real."

"Cheat the eye," he said into her ear, the curls there jumping with her chest, "and *convincere*."

They were pressed closer and closer to a crested doorway where the bartering began with bows and curtsies.

"Look around," their hostess said, "at the envy."

Donatella resisted the suggestion, left to her insecurities again as Princess Doria saw what else Alessandro had brought.

"Benedetto's libretto!" The princess took it, stroking it. "And now he is a Cardinal. You never think when you are children,"

"Did you enjoy *Roma*?"

"Only as I remembered it."

"Ah."

"My dear," the prince spoke up, "there are so many others to greet."

"Yes, yes. They can all wait a moment. I hear you will not perform tonight."

Alessandro looked around as if her attention wasn't enough. "You don't mind?"

"Instead you will play the suitor," She wasn't subtle pulling his arm through Donatella's.

"At your service." He bowed again so Donatella had to repeat her clumsy curtsying.

"My dear friend, you forgot–"

As they turned, the princess was waving the libretto in the air, the prince still making amends to the reception line.

"It's yours. I have a copy."

They entered a room filled with whispers about whether Alessandro had willingly brought Donatella, his proper and improper popularity easily separating them. The hall was lined with golden chairs and pedestal effigies, her eyes cheated and convinced by panoramic walls and skies of flying crystal. She recognized a few cornered musicians as reservedly as they did her, double doors almost hitting her as they opened to let in a long fringed table already set with yellow and blue china, cluttered silver, and rising glass. Hurried motion and disputed positioning threatened to topple its floral and peacock-feathered centerpiece, while a moveable and bannered sideboard swerved to where Donatella thought she was out of the way. Its main monument offered layers of fast-day chicken and vegetables on a base of ship's biscuits, mortared by green sauce oozing over edges of anchovies, olives, and hardboiled egg yolks, topped by a dressed lobster looking down on a circle of oysters and clams. To one side were sculpted mountains of bread, cheese, and fruit, a lion-footed caldron of soup and high-handled platter of rolled meat. On the other a fountain cascaded citrus and wine next to plates of pastries congregated around a cathedral cake.

There was applause for the sudden spectacle, whether or not with confidence that supper's flavors hadn't been compromised for the sake of appearance. Servants pulled chairs to table, everyone knowing their place except Donatella.

"Who is she?" began a conversation for anyone who heard.

"An English sailor's daughter."

"He lives in the same house."

"Oh. Look at her. It can't matter."

Location continued to be important because she wasn't, all eyes on her taking a seat next to Alessandro, although nothing was said that was thought except in the speaking about anything else.

"Savor it," he advised as the minestrone was served.

The overdone garlic and cloves made her eyes water. He picked up her spoon, filling and lifting it to her mouth not opening soon or wide enough so he wiped it with the napkin appearing as if from his sleeve.

"*Buono?*" He tried hypnosis.

She didn't want to look away. "Yes."

The Garibaldis were across the table, Alessandro pretending Maria Caterina was of less interest than Lonati arriving late.

"Signor Stradella, it seems you're pleased with your accommodations," was more the next course than silver serviced mounds of *cappon magro* that steamed and toppled.

"*Molto.*"

"Near wherever you need to be?"

"*Conveniente* and *tranquillo.*"

"All a man requires," Signor Garibaldi broke his silence and some bread.

"Not a little romance?" an unknown lady spoke up.

And another. "A little is never enough!"

"So we share him."

"Like the sunshine."

"And rain."

"As I do," Alessandro didn't know how or care to put an end to such talk, "you all."

The meal continued with eggplant stuffed *braciole,* refills of wine complicated by cheeses and fruits, and the ease with which all the men but Alessandro were ignored. Donatella was glad to eat just so she wasn't seen to be listening.

"*L'oh,* such an appetite." Alessandro's arm measured her waist.

Lonati's violin tried but failed to steal the show, Princess Doria tapping a spoon on her glass. "Perhaps one day soon Maestro Stradella will be intended for something besides our entertainment."

No one would disagree, although they could, especially Donatella, who felt him abandoning her.

"What do you say, signor?" The prince obviously knew what his wife was talking about.

Alessandro laid his hands on the table. "That my *intenzioni* are honorable, for, you see" he leaned back in his chair, "I don't have any."

The princess snapped her fingers and the cake offered deliverance from her miscalculation, a sparkler on top and Lonati's music dancing around it, until Alessandro stepped in, taking the hunchback's violin and making the rounds of all he was giving up if ever he was, ladylike smiles encouraging him to risk more than they would. So, for the last time—or not—he obliged with the longing of one note he wouldn't let go of and then did for the next, something right and wrong about the sight and sound of him walking away, love and hate following him everywhere.

Eventually the room was transformed again, dining table and sideboard pulled out, chairs put into rows too close for comfort. The stage was set for a story a future Cardinal knew how to write for Alessandro to tell through the masked voices of *Apollo* and *Marte, Diana* and *Amore,* with a warning that *if you become idle, you will perish by Cupid's bow.* The princess turned to Alessandro with an obviously serious comment, a kiss of her hand his reply.

The same lips brushed Donatella's ear. "Can you stay awake?"

A little wine wasn't what caused her exhaustion.

"That's all right." He stroked her back, even Anna Pamphilj disapproving. "Rest here, so Golone won't have to carry you home."

They waited just outside the house, in the *Piazza San Matteo,* unseen or deliberately ignored by other guests leaving with reliable servants. Soon the hall candles behind them were extinguished. The rain stopped, the damp pavement encouraging a fog.

"Golone has forgotten again."

"Why do you put up with him?"

"He doesn't cost me anything. Let's go."

She had never been on the streets at that hour. They were tight and loose, empty and full of possibilities, inhospitable and inviting as Alessandro seemed to enjoy them. She wanted to be comforted by him squeezing her fingers and whistling quietly, but was afraid of what was following them.

CHAPTER FOURTEEN

They turned around. Golone was a shadowy figure that could have been anyone.

"Did you bring my cape?"

"You never wear it."

"But I might've been *galante.*"

"I'm not cold," Donatella excused both.

"Neither am I, despite *Torino,*" Alessandro immediately realized he shouldn't have said. "I have faith lightening won't strike again."

"Is that thunder I hear?" Golone couldn't resist.

"No. It's a beautiful night."

"For tramps and thieves."

"And the moon." Alessandro pulled back Donatella's hood and pointed upwards, Golone shaking his head and going on ahead. The alleyway rose like a darkened chimney flue, towards, but not in sight of, the sky.

"It's not there."

Alessandro wasn't patient with her, hurrying them past Golone and around a corner in anticipation of Despina waiting. Sure enough, a door opened before either put a hand to it, a hollow-eyed Nubesta wondering why Golone wasn't with them.

"He's coming."

"Where's my aunt?"

"Gone to bed."

Donatella's expression must have asked the next question.

"She said you are your own responsibility."

Alessandro was the boy who stayed out all night, showing the way to tiptoe upstairs.

"Donatella? Is that you?"

"Yes, Nonna."

"And *Signore Stradella*?"

"Yes."

"Did you enjoy yourselves?"

Donatella went to her grandmother's bed, Alessandro answering from the doorway, "Until *Il Gobbo* arrived."

"*Domani.*" Nonna closed her eyes, still smiling.

Donatella followed him up one floor too many, their association in public not half so daring as into the late night of his apartment, anticipating her aunt calling her out. Alessandro used the only candle burning to light a few others, the curtains also gesturing her to a window so she might view the bay's shipshape stage and beaming impresario of a lighthouse. The sky showed stars, some more celebrated than others. But no moon.

He had opened the window enough for his head and shoulders to lean out. "Unless you do this."

"Please, don't."

"I've got you," he sang as confidently as she didn't feel with her upper body in mid-air, yet obedient to his instruction to look sharply left and up where the nearly full moon balanced on a cloud.

"All right. I see it."

She was pulled in like the curtains, on the coolness of the wind and his maneuvers so she thought he might lie down on the couch with her, as ridiculous a notion as falling for the sight of the moon.

"I hope my aunt didn't hear." She sat up, crossing her arms.

"You're your own responsibility." He removed his coat, folding it on the closed top of the harpsichord, his cravat floating up and down to land there, too.

"She's like that," Donatella felt surprisingly satisfied, "when she isn't listened to."

"She didn't want you to go?"

"She didn't want me asked to go."

"Ah. I was hoping I'd found a rebel in you. Instead you do as you're told or asked."

"I could refuse either."

"Or negotiate between the two." He sat at the writing table. "I need more *vino.*" He stretched his arms out and laid his head down facing her with a brother's benignity.

"I think she sleeps with the key."

"You're light on your feet."

"No."

"If she wakes, you have an excuse."

"I do?"

"Just letting her know you're back."

"She'd be suspicious anyway."

He jumped up. "Especially if you had something else to tell her." He went down to his knees, his arms covering hers in white and his hands praying. "What could it be?" They opened and folded around hers. "I know!" His lips bowed and proposed to her fingertips. "Marry me."

Even a princess would have despaired as he begged Donatella to take him lightly. He sat on the floor propped against her legs, his head tilted into her skirt like a cat in its own space happening to touch upon hers. Bells rang on the hour and candlelight lowered through another. The next thing she knew she was cold and laid on the couch alone, water splashing and Alessandro coming into the room with his hair dripping, shirt open, a towel thrown down to the settee, shuffling slippers taking him to the window.

"Ah. There it is. A halo for the *lanterna*."

"What time is it?"

"Late and early."

"I'm sorry."

"I'm not. Come, see."

He put his hands in her hair as she stood beside him, freeing it all and giving her the pins. "How do you fix it for bed?"

"I braid it."

He made an awkward attempt to separate and weave it. "Are you looking at the moon?"

"Yes."

"Is this distracting?"

"Well—"

"How to secure the end?" He looked around.

She gave him a couple of pins.

"*Là.*" He finished, approving his effort and the small of her back. "Though it might come undone."

"I sleep quietly."

"So you do." He accompanied her to the door of his apartment, checking beyond with more experience than sending a woman off with only her hair tended to. "What will happen if it's known?"

"I'll explain."

"And blame the moon?"

"And your influence."

He pinched her chin.

She looked back from the first steps down to the second floor and could barely see him closing the door very slowly on knowing how far to go with her. The house was as quiet as it should be, but she felt discovered, and, once safely in her room, not herself. Her fancy dress came off when it should, draped over a chair where it seemed to rest as she couldn't, corset and stockings indecently falling to the floor, the looseness of her nightgown too pleasurable. Her journal was open to her feelings but she couldn't put them into words, flickering candlelight imagining what she faced. She paced the room, at odds with herself, unable to think or breathe until she stood on the bed and pushed her small window open.

The air was fresh, the smell of the sea perilous, the wings of a bat making her heart beat even faster. She could see a little of the sky, darker than at midnight, and hear voices below. There were lights here and there, suggesting that for some morning had already come. Or, as she was hesitant and hopeful answering an insistent knock, proving the previous evening wasn't over yet.

"I tried before."

"I was sleeping."

Nubesta looked towards the bed.

"What do you want?"

"It's not so different." The young woman was pale and sweating.

Donatella closed them in. "Are you all right?"

"Are you?" Nubesta was still standing with her back against the wall.

Donatella didn't acknowledge or deny anything.

"Well, it's not often I get more than I bargained for."

"What do you mean? Oh—"

"Oh, oh." Nubesta laughed in tears.

"Are you sure?"

"As you'll never be."

"What will you do?"

"I thought you might help me."

"I won't say anything. And you might hide it a while."

"Forever."

Donatella understood what was implied and even hoped was meant, also wanting to be rid of unhappy consequences. Nubesta sat on the bed and waited, but Donatella was unable to offer more than her patience.

"Get some sleep." The unlucky girl finally left.

A few hours later Despina came out of the breakfast room wondering why Donatella hadn't stay in bed longer considering how very late she came in. Donatella only admitted she would take a nap later, so little said all her aunt wanted to hear.

Nonna, on the other hand, could not create scandal enough.

"Was it wonderful?"

"I wanted it to be."

"He took care of you?"

"I suppose."

"So others noticed?"

"I don't know."

"You do."

"It doesn't matter."

"It does."

Donatella hoped silent strokes with the sponge would quiet her grandmother, too.

"Why are you disappointed?" The old woman always knew where she was going and how to get there. "You couldn't sleep?"

"I had more wine than I'm used to."

"And *attenzione*? But not quite enough."

"There. I'll brush your hair." Donatella couldn't resist a confession much longer.

"You haven't done your own." Nonna's trembling hands pushed Donatella's away. "I used to make curls around your face."

"I had them last night. You saw me."

"I've always liked that dress on you."

"Your jewelry helped."

"And your *Gioconda* smile." Her touch was truly tender. "You did smile?"

There was a commotion in the hall, more movement than noise until Golone said he would get the doctor and Despina called for Cook whose appeal to the Madonna wasn't unusual. Any need of her outside the kitchen was, and Donatella thought of how a few hours earlier a desperate act was hinted at and perhaps even imminent. Then Nubesta's voice joined the crisis, Donatella wondering what and who else was in trouble, still hesitating to find out when Nonna begged especially to ignore her coughing.

"Oh, there you are!" Her aunt suddenly included her niece. "I thought you had gone back to bed."

"I can't do those stairs!" Cook's chest heaved as her eyes climbed.

"Is it catching?" Nubesta panicked. "I won't go if it's catching!"

"He's probably hung over." Despina couldn't talk herself into not worrying, though. "Golone seemed to think it necessary to get the doctor."

Donatella understood. "I'll go up."

"I suppose you should," her aunt surrendered once if not for all.

Cook took charge. "I'll make a basil poultice."

Nubesta was almost forgiving. "I'll find lavender oil."

"Bring up both." Donatella's purpose rose with each step she took.

CHAPTER FIFTEEN

She wouldn't let them bleed him. She remembered her father's longest visit, whispers of how he had been injured, his pain much worse because of her mother's sobs and a physician's assault on his fever through his arm. Yet the only questioning was of Donatella propping up his pillows too soon, his ribs minding as his bruised expression did not.

Alessandro looked bloodless already and slighter in bed than he did on his feet, not asleep or awake, rolling his head and inaudibly moaning. The doctor approved the use of poultices and prescribed laudanum.

"Will you be his nurse?" he asked, without a hint of sarcasm, although she listened for it.

"Yes, of course."

"Refresh the compress every few hours."

"It could last for days," Golone said as a matter of fact.

"Not necessarily." The doctor preferred talking to Donatella. "When he wakes give him a few more drops." He placed a small blue bottle on the table that held the sonnet box on a lower shelf.

"He was so well last night," she murmured.

"You were with him?"

"For some of it."

"Did he drink much?"

"Wine, with supper."

"Nothing unusual then?"

"We ... he was caught in the rain, without a cloak."

"Nothing unusual." Golone wouldn't be ignored.

"Many things trigger these episodes: eating and drinking, even rain hitting the face. They're chronic, not life threatening."

"Except for a style of life," Golone was almost profound.

"Let's hope he'll learn to live for a ripe age. Your challenge," the doctor took her aside, "is to keep him here awhile." He understood her skepticism. "You can do it."

The prison was hers, holding her between friendship and more. Her nursing touched Alessandro's hair as affection shouldn't, stroking it off his forehead, hoping the basil and lemon astringent pulled out the migraine that plagued him like crimes did the guilty. She had experienced enough nursing to know how to do something and nothing, sit nearby and watch for better and worse, read without concentrating, doze but not really sleep. Eventually her aunt offered to relieve her but Donatella also refused to eat, sipping a little of the ginger tea that at least wet his lips, too. He knew she was there and didn't, a slight turn of his head so she caught the muslin from slipping, a sound never quite a word, ripple in his throat, and flicker of eyelashes. But not enough consciousness to recognize what her devotion meant, hour after hour, morning into afternoon into evening, witnessed by Nubesta's coming and going with fresh compresses.

And Golone trying to avoid her. "You haven't given him all the laudanum?"

"No!"

"So where's the bottle?"

Donatella also saw it was gone and Alessandro suddenly noticing them. "How do you feel?" She expected some witticism wondering what the fuss was.

"As if I've been beaten up *ancora.*" He curled his shoulders, arms, and legs into a mound of unsympathetic bedcovers.

Despite Golone's presence she moved the back of Alessandro's nightshirt down and his hair up, applying the sweetly scented treatment to his nape as if it were the most important thing she had ever done.

"*Grazie,*" she thought she heard him say.

"I'll stay with him tonight," Golone decided, admitting a possibility.

Donatella's weariness was old and new, and her coughing as hard as Nonna's, so Despina sent her to the kitchen for something medicinal. She hardly touched a bowl of soup, but Cook insistently wrapped *focaccia,* cheese, and dried olives for her to take with her. There was something Donatella needed to ask Nubesta looking pitiable by the kitchen fire but she couldn't remember what it was. With Cook's parcel under her arm, a bed-warmer against her chest, and the second floor landing not as far as she wanted to go, she met Golone fleeing the responsibility she knew he shouldn't have.

"Is that food for me?" he asked with his hand out.

"What? Oh, take it."

"No wine?"

"No."

"But I have such a thirst." He was already eating, dropping crumbs he swept with his feet.

Donatella watched his return to duty before going downstairs again. "Nubesta?"

Her aunt appeared instead. "The girl's useless."

"Can wine be taken up?"

"Not for signor?"

"Golone. He's sitting with him tonight."

"I'm sure there's no need." Despina sorted through the keys on her wrist, mumbling, "I'll take care of it. He forgets he's a servant, asking for wine, flirting like he has more to offer than trouble. I don't know what Signor Garibaldi was thinking, except to remind me this house isn't my own!"

***

Donatella overslept the chance to be the first to find Golone anything but vigilant on his master's couch. Still, she was glad the doctor had returned to Alessandro sitting up insisting on *caffè forte* and a brisk walk to knock the *demoni* from his head.

"Your nurse has her orders."

"My nurse?"

"What next?" Golone stretched.

"Your jailer."

Alessandro's head dropped into his hands and a slow moan.

"You see." Donatella stroked his pillow.

"Hmm." The doctor picked up the blue bottle that was back where he had left it. "Empty? No more medicine for you, signor."

"I thought it was a spell." Alessandro fell out of the conversation, avoiding the awkwardness he wouldn't have felt anyway, always as if unconscious of his sins and anything surrounding him that wasn't his choosing.

So Donatella stayed, for the unknown and contradiction of those senseless moments. She sat by his bed in the safety of friendship, and even for virtue, rubbing his temples with lavender, knowing she might never have such intimacy with him again, yet missing him for the time it took to recover his genius and foolery. Especially the vitality that made him difficult to keep up with, challenging her to a movement of her own. He rested easier than the day before, but without the flush and agitation he seemed sicker. So the doctor was right and wrong. Alessandro wouldn't die that day or the next, but neither should he lose his life like her grandmother lying in bed or at best sitting in a chair. Better to be removed like the fruit from the tree than ripen beyond enjoyment and fall for decay.

Eventually Donatella did check on Nonna, who had enough strength to command her back upstairs. "The *dottore* looked in and agreed I'm old! *Qui.* Take these two with you. They keep lying on my chest."

"Oh, Nonna, they're devoted to you."

"They'll love Sandro more. What ladies wouldn't?"

Donatella gathered up the cats, one in each arm, struggling with them and the neglect of her grandmother, although her return to Alessandro's room soon eased their argument and her conscience.

"There you are." She heard him without recognizing his voice.

"Where's my aunt?"

"Anywhere but here."

"I just went to check on Nonna."

"Ah. Attentive to us all. But how are you?"

She was touched by the simplest of questions. "Fine."

"You look tired."

"I am, a little."

"Of me?"

She wanted to say more than she did. "Of course not."

"It happens."

She pretended not to wonder how. "Are you hungry?"

"I think I am."

She tried to leave, had never known his hand so cold or warm.

"Ever since *Torino,* such anger gets in my head."

"Shhh." She fussed over him knowing exactly why she did, but he didn't take advantage letting go of her and withdrawing under the covers. "Tell me some other time."

"No. I want to forget."

When she returned with fish stew and bread chunks for both of them he was asleep again, her cats stretched along his side and across his feet as they chose not to see each other. She went into the salon to eat, sitting on the hearth stone and thinking of lighting a fire, not that evening but the next. By then Alessandro might take a pose on the settee, a little meat and wine, and think of music again, regaining his color and presence, enjoying a heat that didn't make him shiver, although it mostly went up the chimney. It was the first time she didn't see signs of composing, no inspired if ordered notations of something new to be heard from him in a month or two. There was a letter started, to a *Most Illustrious and Most Excellent Sir, finding myself short of commands ... permit me to revive your memory of my servitude ... your Excellency should not leave me so idle ...*

She heard a noise and saw her cats claiming his bowl where she had placed it beside her, wagging tongues pushing it to the edge. Nothing was spilled they didn't clean up as well as themselves.

"I've lost my supper."

A robed Alessandro was holding onto the sides of the doorway into the room.

"Should you be out of bed?"

"My legs don't think so."

She helped him to the couch, her cats propping him up. He petted them like she wanted to stroke back his hair.

"I'll get you more."

"I have a servant."

"I can take care of you."

"Like my mother or sister?"

"For you to get better."

"Not just jailer, but a *riformatore*."

"I'm going," she immediately thought she should explain, "for more stew."

"Quickly. Or I'll lose my appetite."

He must be feeling better, back to his old tricks or at least with some energy for reminding her of them, although she didn't tell his other servant the whole of her thought.

Golone hardly listened anyway. "I'm on my way out."

The mood in the kitchen was about Nubesta standing in the darkness of her situation and cape, unlikely Golone was about to do the right thing.

"I've lit a candle." Cook crossed herself in front of the altar she had made on a side shelf of the baking ovens, a cheap statue of the Madonna and Child behind a votive's low offering.

"Will she be all right?"

"There's no saying until it's done."

"My aunt doesn't know?"

"Oh, I think she does. Signor must be better."

"A little."

"Then a bigger bowl. And anise cake for his digestion."

"You sound like Nonna."

"Not when I sing!"

Despina wasn't as spirited in her observation, coming out of the sitting room holding a book. "Do you think he needs you?"

Donatella's arms were already aching with the tray Cook had overloaded. "We're friends, I hope."

"Impossible to remain so."

Donatella didn't want to argue, realizing that one day Despina would be her only relative in the house, city, the future—or maybe not. "Mama and Papa want me to live with them."

"I'll never go."

"I won't leave Nonna."

"Until she leaves us."

"There are other things to consider."

"Like a lodger," her aunt caught the tray from tipping, "needing attention."

Alessandro wasn't patient or impatient, still on the settee, his legs slightly bent, shoulders propped, and head slung back as though the ceiling offered more than molded squares of peeling plaster. The cat on his stomach kneaded the linen where his robe had opened, its sibling brushing her head back and forth on the hand dangling in lazy seduction.

"What? *Genova* hasn't missed me? No invitations for going out?"

"No. Even if it has and there was." Donatella set the tray down on the half empty writing table with no work in progress. "Will you eat here?"

"*Qui.*"

"Then sit up."

"*Scusi, bellezze,*" he repositioned his feline admirers, "your mistress has become mine."

Donatella gave him the bowl and a piece of bread.

"It's fishy." He took a long drink. "Now I know why they stick by me."

Donatella tried to smile at his tolerant battle with her cats.

"Wait your turn." He tried raising the bowl out of reach.

"Bad girls," Donatella intervened.

"And this is your *punizione.*" He made a desperate dip of the bread before putting what was left on the floor. "You don't mind?"

"What?" She realized she was frowning. "No."

"*Così,* what's the matter?"

She felt her heart quickening. "My parents sent me money."

"Not for new clothes?"

"Well, I don't have anything to travel in."

"Ah. I knew it."

"You did?"

"The first time I saw you. That you weren't meant to stay here, either."

CHAPTER SIXTEEN

He was in her hands, or, at least, his nose fell upon them. "Jasmine?"

"Lavender."

"A special cure."

"Yes. No. I mean, it has helped my headaches."

"Where do yours come from?"

She felt herself pulled in, the catch of the day, not wanting to be saved by his letting her go. "I don't get out enough. Or so Nonna says."

"We were changing that." He tried to become smaller. "It's chilly. Call Golone to make a fire."

"He's gone."

"Then Nubesta."

"So has she."

"Ah."

"I can do it."

"No. I can do without it." He slid over on the settee, patting its empty side. A cat jumped up and, with a push, was off.

She sat at his writing table instead.

"I should know by now. It's easy to drop out of the world."

"Only that you must take it slow for a while."

"The *dottore* told you?"

"He didn't need to."

Alessandro groaned and yawned.

"You should go back to bed."

"I never sleep so much."

"Why you got sick." She meant to provoke him.

He didn't mind. "Do you have more lavender?"

"In my room."

"Don't go. Soothe me with conversation." He stretched his legs on the sofa again.

"About what?"

"Anything but your leaving."

She thought quickly. "What will I copy next? A cantata for Christmas? Or madrigals?"

He shivered and closed his eyes. "Soothe me."

She didn't think he realized she had hurried away until she returned with the blanket from his bed, attempting to stretch it over his shoulders and feet, choosing the latter as they were bare. Even the coarse gray wool couldn't make him common and colorless, just availably frail on the elegantly curved couch. He gestured for her to sit against his legs, little space with him there—or anywhere. She might have found comfort in making the most of it, like her cats sharing the day's last sunlight, one small splash from the sea's horizon to the edge of the carpet's shore.

Any moment Despina might knock on the door—or wouldn't bother, discovering what she was looking for. Or in another day or week or month there would be an anonymous letter unlike any other, concerned with the shrinking of his life to fit hers.

"How *prudente* can you be, alone with me?"

She hesitated to think of what she should say. "As I know I am."

"And I do, too." He was separated from her by shadows like a priest hearing confession. "What an unwilling smile."

"Well, I'm Genoese and English."

"Both enjoy my dramas." He sat up, miming the effort of pulling his heart from his chest.

She laughed, then wondered if she should have.

"Ah. That's better."

"I should go."

"Not until you tell me things."

"What things?"

"How to live near the sea yet not drawn out by it."

She felt some cleverness as though it wasn't hers. "Like a snail towards the rain, sheltered and slow."

"And someone just wasn't patient enough."

She remembered a struggle in a fog. "It felt like he wanted so much and so little from me."

"How did you know him?"

"He sailed with Papa for a year or so. They were friends, too, although he was much younger, even like a son to him."

"And you might've made him one *legalmente*?"

"Oh, I don't think Papa wanted that," she lied about the possibility. "Robbie was unreliable."

"Ah."

"Papa always let me spend a few hours on board when in port, up until then a childish thing, a chance to pretend a little."

"*L'oh,* those chances."

"The wind was always blowing on deck, and he'd tie his neckerchief around my hair."

"Who? *Papa?"*

She saw he knew. "Robbie often teased me like that."

"What a shame."

"I didn't encourage anything."

"The flower said to the bee."

"It's you who teases me now."

"Like applause. For the sound of your bright voice."

"His was even more foreign than Papa's, rolling, like the sea, and he did sing and tell stories. And was a good friend." Her enlivened memory became self-conscious. "I thought it was my fault for not knowing why he wanted to walk with me where Papa wasn't looking."

"Not knowing is the most intimate."

"Yes." She wished she hadn't agreed. "Perhaps in youth, anticipation. But age makes naiveté ridiculous."

"Or rare."

"To be so is to be unnecessary. At least, that's how it seems."

The pause wasn't hesitation but conspiracy between a man and his artfulness. "*Così,* what happened? Did he kiss you?"

She hadn't looked at him for some time and wondered if she ever could again. "He tried."

"But you wouldn't let him?"

"Papa," she felt the relief and anger of long ago, "stopped me letting him."

"What did your sailor do?"

"What do you think?"

"And you became plain."

It felt like a blow and she prepared herself for another.

"You misunderstand. I speak of your perception." He pushed his hair back, apologetic for what he wasn't responsible for, which made her feel his awkwardness more than her own. "Circumstances are the rulers of our lives, unless we overthrow their effect. *Sì*, there's risk, whether to our comfort or discomfort, and even *responsabilità,* as your aunt says."

"To answer to ourselves."

"Or pretend we are in control. Like the performance that seems *perfetto* if the audience doesn't know what went wrong."

"Sometimes it can't be hidden."

"Then it shouldn't be admitted. The high note isn't all!'

"But you've pursued it."

"And got headaches."

"Oh, yes."

"So I might find a *rimedio*."

She was embarrassed, as often happened, by his wit and wiles but especially her imagination. "I'm glad you feel better."

"I wouldn't say that."

He didn't let her flee further than taking his bowl to the tray on the trestle. "We should talk more of beauty."

"Were we speaking of it?"

"When you decided it had escaped you." He wobbled as he stood and reached to the table. "Ah. *Torta.* We've been here before. No icing, or filling. Quite plain. For my good. *Ancora, delizioso*." He kissed his fingers and chewed.

"It was Cook's idea."

"She knows beauty is taste."

"Yet she would've been in awe of dinner fit for a prince and princess." She was glad of the chance to mention it.

"Well displayed, well served, the best *ingredienti.* But superior to this?"

Was he just speaking of cake?

"Back to the subject. Why do you paint?"

She went over to the harpsichord, her hand on its cover. "Not for the reasons you write music."

"Tell me why."

"There's so little else I can do."

"To be like God."

"I wouldn't say that."

"No, you wouldn't."

"It seems arrogant."

"And you think humility isn't?" He rose with a contradiction of decency, making sure his robe was closed but brushing her back on his way to sit at the keyboard.

"I never thought." She inched towards him. "Nonna has tried to encourage me to be bolder."

"With what?" He played an arpeggio. "Your paintings? Your smiles? Your longings?"

She almost rested on him, the harpsichord an alternative support. "Perhaps."

He continued playing without thought or purpose other than to be himself again, clear headed and hearted. "And are you encouraged?"

"I also realize my limitations."

"And those are?" His fingers rode the waves of a few stanzas in his head.

"I'm a spinster without looks or fortune or time on my side."

"Or that's your *opportunità*!"

"How could it be?"

He stopped playing. "A chance to look longer and deeper at what attracts you."

She could hardly breathe as if he was holding her tighter and tighter, although they didn't touch, something as cautionary as compelling between them. Unless it was the argument she had been making all along.

"Are you going?"

She couldn't remember what took her from paralysis to her lifting the tray. "Yes."

"Will you return?"

"If you want ... need me to."

"Bring more lavender oil with you." He gathered the blanket from the couch.

She left the apartment, shutting the door and falling against the frame, the tray juggled, still finding it difficult to understand what she felt and was afraid of, wanted and shouldn't have. It seemed impossible to go away from him, even just downstairs. The rest of the world was like the house, quiet enough to have disappeared, nothing or no one to stop her from turning around and continuing the conversation. She went as far as putting the tray on the floor and a hand ready, like a small child standing up independently for the first time not with doubt but inexperience. Suddenly her innocence was an advantage and she believed there was something for her that wouldn't hurt her, say less than it meant or take more than it gave, nothing unwilling unless she was.

Then other doors opened and closed until she wasn't alone with temptation, just frustrated by it, restraint returning to her thoughts, especially in the choice between wondering and finding out. She picked up the tray, her next steps towards the stairs, meeting Golone, speaking first so it was about where he had been.

"It didn't take long."

Golone glanced towards his master's door.

"He's better."

"Good, for I need to sleep. It cost me too much."

"I'll go down."

Nubesta's tiny windowless room off the kitchen was always dark with just a scrap of a candle, and too warm from a crumbling corner of the oven chimney. Cook waved Donatella out before she was in.

"Is it bad?"

Cook crossed herself.

"But it's done?"

"Maybe, maybe not."

"How?"

"How do you ask such things?"

There was a book in Nonna's collection, looked through as many times as avoided. "She must stay in bed?"

"Moving around makes the body think everything is normal."

"Will you watch her?"

"Not to keep me from my work."

"There's nothing else you need do this evening."

"It could take days, even weeks."

"Oh. What will we say to my aunt?"

Cook wiped her hands on her apron. Donatella realized why and turned to Despina.

"I should throw her out as soon as it's over. And what of that scoundrel upstairs?" Despina grinned. "I should speak to signor. Once he's better, of course."

Donatella didn't argue but felt resistance, enough to think that Nubesta be blamed as much as Golone. So no one should.

"Then again, how would it look if his servant was dismissed?" Despina confronted Cook's altar, blowing out the candles. "I hope enough was paid for silence."

***

Once Nonna's weakness was only for men and their music. She was conscious enough to hear that Sandro was improved and to choke out a question Donatella answered as dishonestly as she could, covering her, kissing her cheek, feeling a love that wasn't just for her.

In the hall, Despina needed distraction. "I want to try the English cards your mother sent me. The deck has a queen."

"So you heard from her, too?"

"She wrote down the rules. It wouldn't hurt you to learn."

"I was—"

"Not nursing him still."

"I was going to bed."

"I've already told Cook to bring us some wine."

Donatella didn't always know what to expect from her aunt. In the salon, a fire spitting and chairs already situated across a console table, she read her mother's instructions in the slim light, at least seeing a way out. "It needs a minimum of four players."

"Then we'll have two hands each."

Despina dealt first, until the last card was exposed and taken, Donatella leading, her aunt playing, then Donatella's turn again, a trick won and lost, then another, and another. Finally, Cook brought the wine.

"I wondered where you'd got to." Despina took the jug and glasses. "I hear crying."

"It's started."

The silence of card playing couldn't help but promote some destruction, Despina drinking three glasses to Donatella's one, ignoring the rules, and suddenly throwing down her hand.

"We can never be respectable!"

Donatella was a little disappointed, having actually gotten into playing, not wanting to stop. "Does it matter?"

"Does it matter? What do you think? That we can flush out babies and assist adulterers and not lose our way in this world?"

"I guess the game is over." Donatella got up.

"I'm all you have," her aunt's voice followed her as Donatella left. She considered going into the kitchen, but Cook turned her away.

"Nothing for you to do here."

Donatella went to her room and got ready for bed. Alessandro called for anyone in the house to hear.

He was looking down from the third floor. "This *opera* is badly staged."

"Shhh."

With a shawl over her nightgown, she went up to him with the freedom of indecency like a breeze in her sails after an endless calm. What was wrong was right as he held up his candle for her.

"No one cares for me. *Così,* I must be well enough to go out *domani.*"

"No."

"Then what shall I do?"

"Rest longer."

"*Impossibile.*"

"You could compose."

"Have you got me a *commissione*?" He found her braid neater than the one he had made. "Ah. You would if you could."

"The princess won't forget you."

He shielded his candle as another grew a shadow from the first to second floor.

It seemed they were discovered when Despina realized something was amiss. "What? You're not supposed to be up there."

Alessandro pulled Donatella into his apartment.

"If she looks in my room?"

"You're not there."

"She'll wonder where I am."

"She doesn't want to know that much." A door closed. "She's gone into her own."

"Or wants it to seem so."

"*Alora,* you'd better not go down yet."

She couldn't see what he was thinking and took a chance on his meaning, her face falling to his chest, linen and lace barely coming between them. There was no mistaking a caress of her hip, another in her hair. But what might have been his legs winding around hers turned into loudly purring cats he bent over to stroke.

"What? The way is clear?" he interpreted their chatter and walked Donatella to the top of the stairs.

Her arm stretched back, her hand slowly slipping out of his, the cats racing to her bedroom door, believing she would let them inside.

PART FIVE

THE LESSON

CHAPTER SEVENTEEN

She knew what she shouldn't do. But the harpsichord's graceful frame wasn't the only one within reach.

"I told you, don't lean on anything!"

She was forgiving and forgiven, but mostly frustrated with her voice that felt trapped in her head.

"Sigh."

"Sigh?"

"Like the wind worked into a gale." Alessandro stood up and took her in his arms, his fingers climbing her spine.

Surprise disguised shame as she didn't resist him.

"Most singers won't wear *corsetti*. Haven't you noticed the size of their waists?"

She wondered how he might make fun of her.

"No frowning. Sing and weep. Never frown." He lifted her arms. "Sigh. For me."

She had to admit he was making it easier and easier to do so.

"Keep your arms up." His hands pushed against her diaphragm. "Make it a sliding note, higher, higher," he dropped them from the inflation of her breasts, "with body and voice until you can't feel any difference," to her waist. "Reach from your toes!"

She held on to pleasing him and not just as he wanted her to sing. She was learning, positioned to rise above the inexperience of her voice and fall for the consequence of his instruction, forgetting herself and willing to defy anyone or anything that might prevent her going further. He clapped and returned to the harpsichord, propping a knee on its seat, his fingers leading on the keyboard, his eyes directed toward the lyrics in front of him.

She added them to the tune she wasn't familiar with, either, faltering, like a baby beginning to talk or her father attempting Italian. Alessandro realized he was playing too fast, not patient but willing to accompany her until she could handle it the other way around. She appreciated his tolerance and did her best to show him, slowly putting the words together into melody and meaning, phrases rolling, his encouragement exaggerating her ability.

He conducted with the sway of his head. "Entice! Enjoy! They're not just notes, but many *avventure*, one giving way for the next."

Her breath and soprano's range were reaching their limit.

"Don't struggle. Think of a kiss. Soften your mouth. Open it, lift your tongue."

She understood how he got himself in trouble but also made the best singers.

"No. Birds. Think of how they hold their bodies and announce their throats before they make a sound. They believe they're made for singing. They don't try, don't strain, and don't hang on. They know they have to do it." He gave his hand and heart to the music, remembering a stage warmed by candles and great passions. "Like flying. Or mating. Or dying."

She was silent.

"You're giving up?"

"I need a lower key."

"You don't."

"But ... you said ... the high note isn't all."

"Did I?"

"Yes."

"Sometimes I say things I don't mean." He rose to adjust her posture, gentler maneuvering her head, gliding around her. "But always, the range of a voice is like the heart for *amore*." Her neck was alert to his next move. "According to the available singers or lovers."

Donatella continued to imagine someone walking in, whether a suspicious relation or just reliable and unreliable servant bringing *limonata* or, now it was almost December, mulled wine. A lady would know how to pretend she wasn't compromised by anything than what was supposed and a gentleman would let her have her innocence.

***

"Has Sandro forgotten?"

No amount of sighing could make Nonna stronger, and standing on her toes was long since impossible. Donatella lightly rubbed her grandmother's dry hands before putting them under the blankets.

"Forgotten what, Nonna?"

"The art of *bel canto.*"

"It's his life." Donatella sat on the bed which was becoming roomier and roomier.

Some days Nonna was hardly able to ask for a drink. "He wastes time on *mortalità.*"

"I don't think he's had a commission for months."

"Not even for an *opera*?"

"He doesn't work for the theater now."

"Not for *Natale*? *Natale* is *musica*!"

Donatella meant to ease her. "There'll be something for him to do."

"*Sì, sì.* That's what worries me."

"Try to sleep." At least Donatella might prevent what was happening downstairs from concerning her.

***

"Lidia," Despina was scolding the new maid, "I told you, never answer the front door!"

Donatella rescued the convent-timid child. "The grate in my grandmother's room needs cleaning and making up."

"Yes, mistress." Lidia looked at the floor.

"Signor Garibaldi," Despina finally acknowledged their visitor.

Donatella stepped forward with a sense of ownership that surprised her. "Have you come to see Signor Stradella?"

"I have." He might have made an assumption about her sudden confidence. "He's in?"

She had already swung around to lead the way.

"And alone?"

She knew it was an inquiry that didn't need answering as much as influencing. "Of course."

On the third floor, Golone emerged from his master's apartment with the remnants of lunch on a tray. "You'll find him sleepy but satisfied."

"Giuseppe," sang Alessandro from as faraway as she had ever heard him. "The *teatro* needs me after all."

"Not exactly." The door closed.

Despina wouldn't wait longer for her dinner, Donatella taking it to her in the sitting room,

"What do you think it's about?" Despina was already pouring a second glass of wine, Donatella's pacing the only thing bothering her.

"Work, I hope. Signor Garibaldi has provided for him before."

"Not always as he meant to." Her aunt didn't connect gossip with cruelty. "Perhaps, finally, he wants him out."

"Of this house?"

"And city."

"I'll protest."

"That would make a difference?"

"Others would, too."

"You shouldn't fool yourself."

***

"I'm glad you understand, Sandro." Their landlord was soon downstairs and, as Donatella came out of the shadows, lifting his hand from Alessandro's shoulder.

"Ah. Here's the one to keep me out of the way."

"So I've heard." Signor Garibaldi didn't sound or look convinced.

"As you should be listening." Alessandro played with every situation as if it was a musical composition, limited and unlimited possibilities of notes, styles, and especially outcomes, knowing the accepted forms and appreciating their merit but also how they might be circumvented.

"What do you think?" Alessandro didn't ask permission to intrude where he was welcome and flirt for advice from Nonna.

"Put your *passione* into the *musica.*"

Lidia appeared with the ash bucket.

"What have you been doing all this time?" Donatella immediately regretted her tone.

"One thing, then another." The girl of twelve or thirteen was in tears. "For you, your aunt ... and Cook."

"Who's this?" Alessandro turned in his seat, a hand still on Nonna's cheek.

"Lidia," Donatella told him, and the girl, not yet pretty or plain, blushed before Alessandro gave her obvious reason to.

"Lidia? Who must have *amore costante*?" He looked for Nonna's sympathies again. "A character in one of my early *cantate*."

"I don't know it," Nonna's voice weakened for one reason or another.

The girl also spoke quietly, "There is constancy in God's love."

"Then it's good you're devoted to him." Alessandro squatted by her.

She wasn't about to agree or disagree, realizing who had given her a place in the world that also depended on serving others. She finished cleaning the grate, crisscrossing kindling, piling small logs, striking flint on marble again and again, and blowing sparks into fire.

"The warmth of hell," Alessandro picked up the bucket before she could, giving it to her, "by the hand of an *angelo*."

"I'm just a girl, signor." Lidia curtsied and left.

"No one told me," Nonna tried to sit up, Donatella not knowing whether to help or discourage her, "what happened to Nubesta."

Donatella adjusted her pillows.

"Or shouldn't I ask? Sandro, you know more than you're saying."

"*Signora*, I'm not the only one."

It seemed two silver *scudi* had done the trick, Nubesta's recovery due to the charity of the Holy Mother and Despina. Certainly the latter showed an unexpected clemency, allowing the girl to ease into her duties, even trusting her to go alone to market, assuming she had learned the hard lesson.

Nubesta came back boasting how the boy at the fish stall had missed her.

The next morning she began hemorrhaging and fainted on the stairs, a water jug smashing and her head hitting the railing. Alessandro carried her to bed, yelling for Golone to get the doctor, softening his command for Donatella to take over. Yet he kept a vigil in the kitchen without his usual hunger for Cook's consolations, although wine and more wine wasn't refused.

"Well, besides a concussion, there's a bad infection and not much hope." The doctor wouldn't give any other opinion.

The only blessing was that it didn't take long. The next evening a priest was sent for, then Nubesta's still inviting body was washed, wrapped, and taken by some relatives who accepted coins from Alessandro.

"For my salvation also," he explained when Despina questioned his generosity.

It wasn't enough. He must also pay attention to the censures threatening him, like the one that ended his involvement at the *Teatro Falcone,* if not with another of the manager's interests. Signor Garibaldi was forbearing, offering lodging and continuing to pay for his wife's lessons, until his turning a blind eye seemed complicity, especially to brothers-in-law known for their volatility.

"She isn't your only student."

"There were others."

"Surely you'll find more." Donatella had brought up laundered shirts, noticed the sonnet box was dusty and was wiping it with her skirt.

"Perhaps a large-waisted diva." He hardly humored himself, standing by a window.

"Is there anything I can help you with?"

"My leisure needn't be yours."

Donatella didn't trust his dismissal. "Can't you compose for yourself?"

"Like you paint?" His walking around the room caged her in, too.

"No. There's a difference between diversion and purpose."

"And you won't let me forget that."

Was it possible that for him the necessity in their association wasn't just so copies were done, headaches nursed, and rumors puzzled? Was there anything about her like the light and dark of his profile, Roman and yet undefined, patient but edgy, there and gone, tilting for creation—or for recreation, lips poised to smile or say something too clever, eyes gleaming for life or love or a lark, lifting for success or scandal, the moon or just the swirl of wine in a glass? Was there any kind of attachment to what she offered, believing in him as he hardly believed in himself?

"So what will you do?"

"What do you suggest?"

"Don't give up."

"On *Genova*?" He picked up a lute.

"How did you come by three?"

"They came by me."

"Such a restrained instrument."

"Too much so." He played some new music, or older than her memory of him. "Unless there is the right tension."

The light in the room suddenly changed, needing candles lit and urges given up or in to. For all his baser impulses, Alessandro was noble once more, reminding her of where they had left off, sighing for music if nothing else.

"Over there," he indicated the scattered papers on the table, "a *libretto,*" then tuned the lute close to his ear.

"Is this it? I've never heard it. What you were playing?" She tried to uncurl the title page. "*Accademia d'Amore.*"

Donatella sat, words and wisdom feeding her like a gently flavored meal, satisfaction as slow and subtle as the melody Alessandro was remembering.

"I was too kind with this."

"It's simply lovely."

"Then it was too kind to me."

"What part will I sing?"

"There's no question."

"I just want to please Nonna."

"No one else?" He propped the lute on the settee, finding the answer under her hand. "I might've written it for you."

CHAPTER EIGHTEEN

There were woundings all the time. In words or actions, owned or anonymous, answered or ignored. Sometimes they were as obvious as Pier Francesco Guano attacked on the second of December, needing twelve stitches on his face. Lonati must have known it was old news, pounding the front door and rushing upstairs.

"Only the beginning." He didn't acknowledge Donatella dropping music sheets, just Alessandro picking them up. "Beware. If you don't turn around you're a dead man."

"Or spared by the *magia* of *musica*."

"Changing assassins into *aficionados*? That never happened."

Alessandro put his arm across Donatella's shoulders. "It's almost dinnertime. Go see what there is."

"Chicken pie."

"Ha! How clever."

"No." Donatella wished she could take credit for a witty remark. "I helped roll out the pastry."

"You laugh. You forget." Lonati was at least shaped to charge like a bull, and for ducking under Alessandro's arm. "And don't know." He grabbed Donatella's as she tried to get away, really afraid of him.

"Please," she pleaded of Alessandro, too.

"Are you crazy," he pulled Lonati away but saw it wasn't enough to defend her, pushing a hand under the other man's chin, tightening his cravat and face, "handling a woman like that?"

Lonati shook free, stumbling into the hall of the apartment and Golone, who he was sure would understand. "At least I handle the ones that don't matter."

Golone agreed only that he should leave.

Lonati ignored him. "I was made to look down."

"Mostly into the gutter." Alessandro returned to the harpsichord, Donatella nearer to tears than resuming their practice.

Lonati tried conciliation. "What about our little group?"

"I prefer to be on my own."

"Certainly in glory."

"You can have it all." Alessandro's irritation came down on the keyboard, but then he played the piece as pleasantly as it was written. "I'm a prisoner of *cortesia* now."

Lonati snatched the pages out of Donatella's hands. "Well! This is from the good old days. Rome, mid-sixties? All carnivals and palaces, especially for Monesio and Stradella."

"What's behind us may be all there is." Alessandro continued to accompany his aggravation with music that might soothe it.

"Your singing was also magnificent."

"What part?" Donatella approached the conversation.

Alessandro winked. "*Rigore,* of course!"

"The talk of the town," Lonati began to pet her arm but thought better of it, "before he received more attention for his lack of discipline."

"How was that?" Golone put his feet up on the settee where his sitting was already out of place.

"You ask because you know," Alessandro found another reason to scold him. "Where are you going?" he noticed Donatella leaving.

"To see about dinner."

"Not for me. I must get out of here." His arms pushed the room and her influence away, the other men actually hesitant to follow him out.

Donatella wandered around the apartment looking for something to ease another rejection. Silver and gold weren't the value she had in Alessandro, an empty bottle and glass more enemy than friend, music organized and disorganized on table and chair and couch not enough to know about him. Harpsichord, lutes, and violin might regret his distractions with more reason than she had, made for what should never be forgotten about him. She picked up a shirt from the bed and stockings from the floor, lifting them towards her face and laying them over a chair in case they were worn again before Golone brought them downstairs. A dressing gown drooped inside-out over a bedpost had light and dark hairs and the faint scent of lavender on its collar. One velvet slipper peeked from under the bed, so she got on her hands and knees to join it with the other. She knew the wardrobe was neater than he was, with more shirts than required since he wasn't in demand, the finer ones too long unworn and needing freshening, like fancier coats and trousers hung down the left side where shoes dulled by dust couldn't take them where they were meant to go.

Of course, there was that little treasure chest, still beside his bed and locked, hopefully the key where it used to be.

"Signor went out in a hurry," her aunt announced, startling her. "What are you doing?"

"Tidying."

"Get Lidia to—no, I don't want her up here."

"Golone is lazy. You know that."

"Golone is ... never mind." Her aunt waited for her to leave the apartment first. "You should be with your grandmother."

At least when Donatella's mother had gone away, Nonna was there to talk and live in the house with despite Despina's moods and malice. Now her grandmother didn't speak, not even through her eyes, and barely lived. Lidia took good care of the sleepy signora while Donatella performed a final act of devotion, not altogether altruistically, avoiding Nonna's demise, less culpable if Alessandro made a more confident singer of her yet.

The doctor came and went. "Try to keep someone with her. She's not the kind to die alone."

Trembling, Donatella accompanied him to the gate.

"How is your other patient?"

"Impossible."

"A malady I can't treat.

Back in the house, Despina seemed emotionless even as she wiped her eyes. "Lidia can stay with her during the night."

"No, it's my place."

"The girl used to nurse the old nuns. Of course, she's needed for other duties, too. Then you and I can take turns, though I don't think for long."

Donatella was never far from Lidia keeping vigil over Nonna, the girl murmuring prayers while making up the fire, stroking the old woman's hair, or curling into the big chair with the cats easily fitting in with her.

Eventually, Lidia acknowledged Donatella was there, sitting just outside the room. "She's whispering 'Sandro'."

It was almost midnight when Alessandro and Golone returned, trying and not trying to be quiet. Donatella hurried to greet them.

"This house is depressing." Golone sat on the stairs.

"Wait." Donatella couldn't stop Alessandro rushing to her grandmother's bed and kissing lips that suddenly knew what was happening.

"She's trying to say something," Lidia offered. "You have to listen closely."

Alessandro put his ear to her mouth. "What? I'm drunk?"

"She's right," Donatella snapped.

"As always, on *vita*."

"Well," Despina had taken the time to dress but not see Nonna's smile. "What a thing to say to a dying woman."

Lidia backed into the shadows, Alessandro realizing what had really done harm, smoothing Nonna's hair.

"I'm sure the neighbors will notice our lights at this hour."

Alessandro motioned Donatella over and left the room, so her grandmother had nothing to breathe deeply for, her eyes losing the struggle to stay open, her lips too shriveled to have ever been kissed. Lidia coaxed them to sip a little milk while Despina sank into the big chair, bowing her head.

Alessandro was soon there again with violin and music.

"Now?" Donatella understood.

"The chance we have."

"Should we send for a priest?" Despina stood up.

"No." Donatella reached towards her grandmother. "She's just having a bad night. It's too warm in here." She wouldn't admit the coldness of Nonna's cheek, just what she could never forgive herself for. "Lately I've neglected her." She primped the lace on Nonna's hollowed neck, smoothing the quilted satin that gave some shape to what was below, but feeling the waste.

Beauty was cruel, especially to itself. Donatella collapsed forward, wondering where Alessandro had laid his violin, a strange consideration in all the embarrassment and satisfaction of his body over hers as he returned the shawl to her shoulders.

"What's this?" Despina had to be noticed. "Signor, please! Send Golone for a priest." As far as she was concerned, Alessandro was tuning his violin and hearing nothing else. "Let it be on your conscience."

Donatella stood with a vengeance for her aunt's meddling, Alessandro very discreetly shaking his head.

"Can't we do something proper in this house?"

"All right," Donatella wasn't answering her.

Alessandro leaned over her grandmother again. "*Cara signora,* heaven is in your darling girl's voice."

"I don't think she can hear."

His shoulder and chin offered the violin to its bow already playing the air, the tenor of his singing also finding the perfect pitch for what was to come:

Chiedi al niente il tutto! il sèmpre al mai!
E à l'impossibil che possibil! che possibil fi…a.
Ciò che chiedi, impetrat forse portra…i…,
Ma a rigida beltà, che amore obli..a…
Se tu chiedi piet… à…, Se tu chiedi piet…à…
Non, non l'otterra…a…a…a…a…i…i.

The voice of experience grew intense with *Discipline* offering the hindsight of asking all from nothing, always from never, possibility out of the impossible, without a hope for pity from unyielding and love demanding beauty.

A violin solo continued Alessandro's introduction to Donatella's part.

She quietly cleared her throat and wiped her eyes, remembering how it was all right to sing and weep, and also her bearing, feeling the freedom of her nightclothes and positioning of her slippered feet on a stage that would never make her famous.

Le donne più bel…le, crudeli rubel…le,
Ingrate son tu…u…u…te…e…e, Ingrate son
tu…u…u…te…e…e

She saw the teacher in his eyes and softened the high tessitura, controlling the throat's rolling and insisting:

Ingra…aaaaaaaaaaaaaa…te son tu…u…te…

Taking a breathless breath for the heart of the argument:

Regna la Cortesi…a, Regna la Cortesia sol..ol..ol
nelle bru...te…

That only in plain women does courtesy prevail:

Regna la Cortesi…a.., Regna la Cortesia

Sol…ol…ol nelle bru...te,

Sol…ol…ol nelle bru...te…

Her first and uncertain trill sent the violin on a lengthy lyrical agreement so she almost missed a cue:

Mediocre bellezza già mai di fierezza

Non arman le stel…el…el…le…,

Non arman le stel...el…el…le…

No…ooooooooooooooo n'arman le stel...el….le

And felt the relief a mediocre woman should, if truly without arrogance:

Regna la crudeltà, Regna la crudeltà

Sol…ol…ol nelle bel…le…

For a happy and unhappy conclusion:

Regna la crudeltà…

Regna la crudeltà…

Sol…ol…ol nelle bel…le

So…ol…ol nelle bel…le…

Her final trill felt better than the first. She was also surprised her aunt didn't scold Lidia and Cook for peeking into the room. But it wasn't the time to be pleased. Violin and bow dropped to Alessandro's sides, Donatella to her knees by the top of the bed, Despina at its foot, while Lidia whispered the rosary and Cook tried to pray but was soon sobbing instead. One cat and then the other did what the priest hadn't come in time for, washing Nonna's forehead, cheeks, and even lips.

CHAPTER NINETEEN

She would never sing again. Nonna was laid out through the next day, buried at first mass the one after that, *Santa Maria Maddalena* waiting for more and more footsteps quieting in its divided nave. Despina was impressed by the lowering of fine black velvet onto rear pews so that late arrivals had to sit further up. Donatella only saw who had come for their own sake, veils and heavy wigs concealing identities but not the inattention and hope that the service would be brief. Cook sitting beside her was a little diversion before Alessandro's dedication from the *Cantoria* was the main attraction.

Every lip opens to a smile, and every eye closes to tears.

A heart not beating must be preferable to one breaking. There was cruelty in a man's beauty, too, particularly when he sang like an angel and a fallen one at that. Alessandro was as affecting in gold and theatrics as the priest at the altar, perched even higher and more observed.

Every word becomes song.

Some might say the selection from a Christmas *cantata* wasn't suitable. Nonna would have approved, even Alessandro's ulterior motive. A performer always had to have a next performance.

Nonna once said that when she worked more at swallowing than singing her life was over.

Donatella disagreed then as now, for even bedridden her grandmother wasn't confined to being useless, sharing the time of her life and only asking for the return of her audience of one. Donatella was spoiled with gifts not given for contentment but curiosity and conceit, playfulness, possibilities, wit, wisdom, and mistakenness, too. *If you don't limit yourself, nothing will limit you.* For a long time Nonna knew what she was talking about, even reduced to whispers, covered with clouds, losing her way in the world, fading but only like the sun promising to rise again.

Now Donatella was the one lost, without compass or courage, tossed from thought to thought, afraid to look into the depths, waiting for the next wave to throw her over. *Do it before it's done to you—jump in and you may rise to the top, and like a pearl in an oyster be washed ashore, caught up, discovered, valued and admired* was the advice she had thought she wouldn't need. Yet she wanted to hear more of what she could never do or be, another day or week or month of saving memories, the cruelty of death not the end of the future but a longer past.

She took communion, ignoring the rest of the mass although she knew when it was over, turning and lifting her plain veil. Signora Garibaldi was leaving her husband to make his condolences alone, Alessandro obviously following her out into the drizzly morning.

He had promised to go into the crypt but there Donatella stood unprotected from her aunt, chilled by the air and their relationship.

"Your mother should be here."

"How could she know when to come?"

"She should never have left us."

"She did what she had to."

Despina lowered her head so the priest would see her solemnity, although the moment he was preoccupied she retorted, "As you will?"

Donatella wanted to stop her aunt stepping forward to touch the grainy coffin propped in front of its eternal drawer.

As she turned from doing the same, Alessandro had finally kept his word, her weeping quieter against his already dampened coat.

"Such a display." Despina couldn't wait to escape through the awkward grouping of Cook, Golone and Lonati, Signor and Signora Garibaldi.

"I'm so sorry." Maria Caterina put out a hand that stroked Alessandro's arm. "I hear your mama was a great beauty and singer."

"Her grandmother," Signor Garibaldi corrected. "I remember as a boy. She was lovely, with a voice like yours, Sandro, not for fashion but expression."

"I knew when I met her," Alessandro held Donatella's arm tighter, "I was born too late."

"Fortunate for her," Lonati mumbled.

Maria Caterina put on her gloves. "Money is why you do anything, Guiseppe."

"Please," the priest was a shepherd more for motion than guidance, "I have three yet this morning!"

"Sounds grueling." Lonati's grin suggested he might have said something worse.

"*Grazie, Padre*." Alessandro stepped between them. "Your church is a true treasure of *Genova*."

"Ah." The priest lowered his eyes like a flattered woman. "Thank you, signor. You'll do our Christmas Eve service, won't you? Signor Garibaldi can make sure of it."

"He will." Maria Caterina decided.

"We'll see." her husband was as transparent.

"Your pleasure is mine." Alessandro seemed to mistake what was being arranged.

The Garibaldis were soon gone in the carriage waiting in the square, not offering anyone a lift, so Despina went on ahead with an independent stride. The rain had stopped, although the sun was still absent unless Donatella thought of how close she was to Alessandro. His other arm comforted Cook.

"You will have breakfast, won't you signor?"

"You've made it *speciale*?"

"Oh, yes." Cook became even shorter under his gaze. "I didn't know how many to count on."

"Your talents won't be wasted," Alessandro assured.

"I invited the Garibaldis, but they won't come."

Donatella also declined breakfast, withdrawing into Nonna's room, which was empty full of books, poorer for its cache of expensive jewelry, silent despite echoes, and sadder than anywhere that had known less happiness. It offered death and burial for her, too, cold and dark. She refused Lidia's offer to light a fire or open the curtains or at least smooth out the sheets and blanket thrown across the bed. The cats were the only creatures allowed to stay and more comfort than a Venetian glass rosary found where Nonna had kept it for memories, not prayers. Whether Donatella slept, cried, thought of how she couldn't go on or eventually would, time was the enemy defeated by surrender and disappearing without her participation. Feelings were friends as long as they kept their distance and didn't expect her to forget one for another. Confusion offered no choice but to continue in it, regrets inventing themselves, and sacrifice nothing more than giving up impossibility.

She was determined to grieve forever, every symptom a setback to recovering even a little, her suffering dependant on keeping the door shut on any concern more welcome than not.

Lidia was a persistent angel, bringing a nightgown for Donatella to change into, sponging her face and brushing her hair, making the bed and tucking her into it, at least stirring the hearth to be less dismal. By late afternoon, Cook also kindly intruded with a *pesto minestrone* she always claimed could warm the heart as well as the body.

"My pet," the old woman said as she hadn't for years, "please eat a little."

"You sang so beautifully," Lidia thought was a good thing to mention.

"She should be in her own room." Despina followed them in.

Alessandro was dressed and scented for going out. "This is hers now."

"Signor, I don't think it is—"

"My *affare*? I make it so."

"I'm going to speak to Signor Garibaldi. About another tenant."

"Not Lonati!"

"I don't know who. But it could mean extra income."

"For Garibaldi."

"He'll see us right."

"I'll pay you more."

Donatella tried to sit up to see what she was hearing.

"May I ask for what?"

"No." Donatella almost fell out of bed towards her aunt, Lidia coming between them.

"You don't think of money, my girl. You never have." Despina accused.

"You won't starve," Donatella's will was stronger than her voice, "or turn Nonna's room into profit."

"What will you turn it into?"

Cook was daring. "That's not right."

Lidia gave up one cause for another. "Come on." She hooked Cook's arm. "Your bread will burn."

"Ah, it smells well done." Alessandro stepped into the argument. "How much will it cost me?"

"Signor, I can't take your money."

"*Allora,* you can't take any man's."

Despina hardly conceded. "Well, she can stay here for now."

Donatella sank away from a conversation that didn't include her.

"Until she sails away," Alessandro wasn't pleased to say.

"Oh, she's not going anywhere," Despina considered whether to explain, "while you encourage her."

"*Bène,* we'll see."

"Perhaps you could get her to eat, too." Despina left, taking Lidia with her, not closing the door.

The girl was soon back. "The bread didn't burn. I'll bring you a slice."

"And for me," Alessandro pleased her. "Dripping with oil."

Lidia was a little giddy as she went out, Alessandro taking off his jacket and sitting on the bed, the back of one hand pressed on Donatella's cheek. "Speaking of oil, where is that lavender?"

"Gone," seemed the only word she could remember.

"Wasted on me?"

Donatella closed her eyes, seeing his features still.

"*Scuse.* You need to sleep."

***

"I thought you were going out," Donatella said after a few moments that might have been hours. Alessandro was sat in the large chair, his legs crossed, shoes off, hunched over the journal she hadn't hidden well enough under the cushion.

"I thought so, too." He didn't look up.

She saw the dish on the table by the bed. "Did you get yours with oil?"

"And cheese."

She wasn't glad he had left her some without showing more interest in her eating. "I lie here as if Nonna never did," she said, pushing down the covers.

His reading continued to hold his gaze. "Because she did."

"But I'm nothing like her. Even in her bed and left with her things, a pretender."

He nodded, seemingly more for what he read than heard.

"Yet I hang on. Like a child to a favorite fairy tale. Not for its moral but make-believe."

"So why complain," his challenge wasn't harsh, "if you've lost nothing of her imagination?"

"But what good is it? Imagining what I'm not made for? Does it create anything but disappointment?" She didn't want him to see her cry again. "Though if I don't, what is there to do? Why eat or drink, dress, or think of going anywhere, even just on as before?"

"Someone might hope you had a reason."

She felt a blush of pleasure, then discovery, as he recited words he made his own: "To love for the sake of being loved is to use love up in hope and despair. To love for the sake of loving is to be always in its company, never tiring of its conversation or worrying over its silence, to know it can be given without being given up."

It should have been a shame to be found out like that, those few words resonating beyond fantasy and friendship to a sense of intimacy with the kind of man she should never have had a chance with. He was hated and loved, while she was harmless and irrelevant; music his eternity, silence hers; beauty belonging to him in so many ways but denied her in all but foolishness.

He remained in the chair, a distance between them even with secrets revealed, too much akin in understanding to be anything but sister and brother.

"I'll tell Golone to move your things."

"Perhaps Despina is right."

"Now I know you're feverish."

"I don't want to fight with her."

"Then ignore the argument."

"Is it that simple? To get out of trouble?"

Alessandro approached. "No." He sat on the bed again, still merely companionable, and placed her journal beside the plate of bread and cheese, creating a perfect still life.

She shivered.

"Don't be cold." He pulled the covers up to her neck, demonstrating the effortlessness of mouths touching, then again, coming down for another chance like enjoying the scent of a flower longer the second time.

Suddenly he changed his mind, even before Lidia was standing in the doorway with the fire bucket pulling her down.

"There's a visitor for you, signor. A lady," she really informed Donatella.

Donatella wasn't sure she heard an apology before his coat and shoes and suggestion were gone, at least Lidia caring that she still hadn't eaten.

Why are we ever hungry? Donatella left unspoken.

"Could you light a candle for me here?"

The girl did so, picking up Donatella's journal, the candle's flame illuminating her curiosity for what such private pages might confess.

CHAPTER TWENTY

It was too late. Lidia had learned to read at the convent, forming opinions on more than Donatella's musings.

"You should've stopped him. Whatever it took, you should've stopped him."

The girl must have been speaking of restraint, not romance, although nothing was certain since Alessandro had come along, music most of him, misbehavior least, at times the opposite, his extremes and in-betweens all agreeable, at least with himself. Admirers and adversaries both mistook his confidence, gambles, and escapes, enjoying and begrudging him without meeting his full character. There had been a lady or two who took some time from him, but where were they now except not caring for him?

Was Maria Caterina really a threat, married and yet coquettish, with her gold neck, styled hair, and small waist, power and powerlessness? Her clothes were as fine as a princess', her husband once richer, her behavior less controlled. *Le donne più belle, crudeli rubelle ....*

Lidia was still waiting for Donatella to need her, especially as a confidant.

"Can you get me some wine?"

"Wine?"

"Yes."

"I'm not allowed."

"Never mind."

"And you haven't eaten. I didn't eat for a week after my mother died."

"Oh." Donatella was glad the girl turned away. "Was it long ago?"

Lidia nodded.

"And your father?"

She shrugged. "He went to sea."

"And he sent you to Our Lady of the Mountain?"

"It's what I wanted, but he stopped paying."

"You're welcome to read anything here."

Whether or not Lidia agreed, temptation would weaken her, at least for books with more interesting content than covers, new words to learn and thoughts to assess, feelings turned over and over, everything known and supposed and imagined before her eyes. They would bring her to adventure if not adventure to her, and she wouldn't forget what she had read, although she might chose better or worse. Donatella looked up the walls of them, noticing cobwebs feather dusting hadn't reached, like weak minds only grasping what was effortless.

Suddenly she was tired of lying in bed and walked around the room, wondering how she could make it her own without changing anything. Nonna's space in that house was as perfect as in her heart, cool and warm, light and dark, full of music and lyrics, daring to remember and believe, beautiful and courteous.

She was almost hit with the door as her aunt burst in. "He's with her here. Can you believe it? What's he thinking?"

"Upstairs?"

"No. In the sitting room."

A little relief was better than none. "In a way, it's hers."

"Not to be with him."

Agreeing only made Donatella sadder.

"I can't hear what they're saying. I don't want to know," her aunt lied. "How can this not get back to Signor Garibaldi?"

"How can it?"

"I'm not stupid. A carriage brought her. And her servant waits in the hall." Despina moved aside with the door, a dark cloak standing near and facing up the stairs.

"Golone, what's going on?"

Maria Caterina's lady was startled, Golone descending and smiling, laughter emerging from an even more inappropriate meeting.

"This house is in mourning," Despina reminded weakly.

Alessandro was begging her pardon, gesturing that his visitor should do the same.

Maria Caterina didn't appear to mind. "I appreciate your discretion, signorina."

Despina was, as always, impressed with anyone above her situation.

Donatella was besieged by what she saw and felt, in a state of unhappiness and undress, retreating from the attention and slight of Maria Caterina's sympathy and Alessandro's dilemma. Despina soon invaded her withdrawal again, pacing, sitting, standing and tugging at her sleeves, telling Donatella less than she already knew.

"That man never learns," concluded her commentary on Alessandro helping Signora Garibaldi into her carriage, even kissing a hand she nearly left behind.

"You shouldn't have watched."

"I'm sure I'm not the only who did." Her aunt's shoulders and head dropped as if something had fallen on them, "My nerves, my nerves," and crushed her into the chair. "This isn't an easy time for me either."

Donatella softened. "I know."

"Why do you want this room?"

"It wants me."

"How ridiculous. It's depressing. I don't intend to stay in this house."

"What do you mean?"

"Nothing." Despina changed her mind, at least about telling, leaving the room but not Donatella's listening. "Oh, signor, I thought you were going out."

"No, I need supper. Ah, Lidia, what do you offer? Tea? Milk? No. *Vino. Scuse.* You meant to hide it."

"Where did you get it?" Surprisingly, Despina didn't take the bottle away from Lidia.

"Ah. She cannot lie. *Così*, she doesn't say."

Donatella slept better for a few sips of wine, waking once in the night, drinking a bit more so she wasn't unsettled for long. By morning she was at least ready to compose the letter she started again and again, knowing that even soon finished it might be a month before it was received and read, by then its careful words less forgiving. Her mother might expect the news but not what it exacted, whether regret or blame or, especially, helplessness. It must already be cold in Oxfordshire, damp, too, sunshine lost and found and lost again, snow a surprise before January, days shorter than their dwindling hours. Not so different from *Genova* except the weather was talked about like an unpredictable person, especially in a small village where little else happened. Certainly no scandals or stabbings, if plenty of whispers and wishful thinking. She loved her mother's mischievous writing. All grievances were set aside when her letters came three or four times a year, although it was hard to enjoy the last few written completely in English. Her father had taught Donatella a little to say but not enough to read or write.

Her mother's correspondence took Donatella where she had never been: another world of women finding courage and love and ideas expanding with their territory. They were ships making it further than delicate masts and swaying hulls were built to, beyond the shelter of convention, proving that going to the ends of their earth wasn't prevented by distance but by standing still.

Donatella dusted the letter and waved it like a handkerchief of surrender or farewell. If it could travel on trust to reach its destination, why couldn't she?

***

Alessandro held out the folder she hadn't touched for months. "Nonna would want you to do it."

"If I can stop trembling."

"Then stop drinking."

"It helps me sleep."

"But doesn't take the sorrow from your cheeks."

She touched them without thinking to, her fingers on strings connected to his maneuvers.

"We mustn't cease our *collaborazione*." He opened the curtains in a dramatic turn. "Can you work here?"

"Can you get singers this late?" She was sorry she sounded harsh.

"If not, you and I will sing it."

"I won't." Finally she accepted the music for Christmas and reconciliation. "Anyway, there are too many parts."

"It will be abbreviated."

Golone brought in her painting trestle and top clumsily, the cats almost tripping him.

She wouldn't let him put it down until it was positioned as she directed. "The light is little better than I'm used to."

"You'll need help with the dressing table." Alessandro responded to Golone's grumbling.

"I've cleared it." Lidia entered with the important tray of inks and quills. "I'll bring down your clothes, too. And anything else I can carry."

Alessandro slapped a hand on Golone's shoulder. "Why can't you be so attentive?"

"Because I came freely." Golone shook it off as if the lightest of shackles.

"Scoundrel. We both know. You have a price."

***

Donatella couldn't refuse what was in front of her, holding a pen as if for the first time and chance of happiness for the last. It should have been easy to replicate a well done if yellowing copy, no creative scrawling and scratching out, yet she practiced before committing to the page. *Ah! Troppo è Ver. Ah! Troppo è Ver. Ah! Troppo è Ver ...* the ink flowed across the parchment, a star across the sky disappearing into white instead of dark. Strange that she thought of stars before reading them everywhere into the piece. She duplicated parts of the *cantata,* limited to a performance pulled together in less than three weeks, the most renowned singers and musicians already committed to more lucrative if less exciting Christmas engagements. Its very subject was a story of the incredible, inspired as much by myth as miracle, with corruption and devotion its theme. So while she almost smeared *Lucifero's* base cry of obstruction, not even his fury prohibited the immaculate surrender of the *Maria Vergine* only emulated by the grace of notes and words at stained fingertips. Donatella's writing took on new meaning, a long sweet moan, passion entering her soul and giving reason for expectation and especially the challenge of the struggle between faith and falling for flattery. It couldn't be she was randomly chosen or meant to be ill-used. She was on a journey to find the gift of acceptance more gratifying than doubt, to grow into someone special, beauty truly in the eyes of the beholder, a kiss as much about constancy as betrayal.

The music slipped from her hands; she felt respect and regret for the secret of her relationship with it.

"Lidia won't go if you don't."

Travelers through her life had spoken of the *Presepi Viventi* staged elaborately in *Roma* or *Napoli,* or simply when peasants gathered in a town or village marketplace. *Santa Maria Maddalena* displayed a nativity in front of its main altar, still-life figures in satiny marble, the holy family ignoring those who arrived to bow and marvel, offer gifts already given, and point to unseen stars, donkey and sheep neither tethered nor free. Alessandro had the idea for Lidia to replace the stature of Mary, draped all in white, her lovely hair tumbling from her veil to frame a tranquil expression, the worshippers unaware of her breathing until the soprano had sung *Sovrano Mio Bene.* The priest finally agreed when he saw the girl's pale eyes, closed lips, and immature body, and she was willing—as if she had a choice—because her humility would be on display as someone else's.

***

Despina had gone to a different service of worship as future prospects invited, a ride in a darkly elegant carriage seemingly all she had ever prayed for. Donatella and Lidia walked to church behind Alessandro and Golone, the night arriving with them in the *piazza* where not all ladies were as virtuous approaching the crumbling Romanesque façade of the church.

Alessandro laughed them off. "Look who is here for *il Gobbo*!"

Once inside he was reverent in words and music, bowing to the altar and then to musicians and singers, although he claimed they were less than he required. For the Mass' entrance procession violins dueled without contest in *Sinfonia,* Lonati soloing unrecognizably with emotion and grace, Alessandro running off with the notes on *obbligato* harpsichord. His musical, if not physical, challenger inveigled him back with such fine expression it must be imitated, a perfect opportunity for Alessandro's virtuosity with the ease of a hawk flying high and low and landing on a pause. Lonati let down his guard, face gloomy, shoulders sinking. After a few bars the duo matched their humors again, Lonati's self-pitying relieved by Alessandro's company, connecting their past differences for a chordal, if short-term, agreement.

After the Liturgy of the Word the *cantata* resumed, introducing the cast and their story. First the devil in protest and fury then the *concertino* for an *angelo* and *concerto grosso* with Alessandro taking the part of the *pastore,* Lonati's strings only encouraging the thoughts of the tenor in *arpeggios* and *adagios*.

Lidia played her part well. The altar tapers flickered, smoke floating downwards to mystify her appearance and that of the *prima soprano,* who wasn't the prettiest Alessandro had ever employed. At the heart of the performance the obviously experienced singer rose to the violin's challenge, her breath strung along on Lonati's long phrasing and jumping to follow Alessandro's rapid handling of the keys. As always he enjoyed such alternation, as well as the success of Lidia lifting her head and the *Gesùs Bambino* from the crib. After the Blessing of the Sacrament, there was Communion and the mass' last rituals, the congregation still on their knees, the madrigal singers standing first. Bells rang from the tower, envisioning and extolling. Belief was sustained in countering ways yet harmonization reached out through the nave and ascended the dome, proclaiming that at least for the life of such music heaven was closer than hell.

PART SIX

THE DEPARTURE

CHAPTER TWENTY-ONE

She took a step back. The *Galleria degli Specchi* was an icy hall on fire, forever melting in crystal drops, self-admiring wall to wall and in the high shine of the floor. It was still a long way from one golden end to the other, but reflection had a different meaning.

"Come closer, *signorine.*" Alessandro didn't leave Despina uninvited, if just to provoke her refusal, bowing to Donatella. "You will."

She also moved towards one of many elongated mirrors in between lighting clusters, a splash of wax falling on her barely sleeved shoulder.

Alessandro brushed it away but not before it caused a mark and some pain. He got the attention of a very adolescent page. "Have you some remedy? The *signorina* has been burned by inferior candles."

It seemed the whole room was watching, not believing, but hoping, too, except those who could never side with him, frowning at Donatella insisting she was all right.

"What I wanted you to see." Alessandro struck a pose with her on his arm, the view of herself only improved because he was part of it.

"Should we enjoy the show tonight, signor," he was asked, the tone approaching belligerence, "or find it too serious?"

"It's not my *composizione.*"

"But you may still be of interest."

"I hope so."

"Nothing more active?"

"Not this evening." Alessandro sought Donatella's listening through a glance.

"But there will be others."

"*Bravo*. What reasoning, *Signore Lomellino.*"

"And yours?"

"To take a breath."

"As if your last?"

The questioner was joined by another like him in looks if not bluster. "Careful, Baccio."

"No." Alessandro enjoyed any uncertainty in their chain of command. "My first."

"He's an Aries." Donatella remembered the Zodiac room.

Alessandro lifted his head and heels. "How much you know."

"Only if you tell her everything."

Giovanni Battista hardly needed reinforcement. "Well, well, you've riled Domenico now."

"It's just that," the other Lomellino was obedient, "our sister hasn't spoken of you recently."

"Why should she?"

"Well. She thinks so much of singing," Domenico tried to be clever and condemning, "which is the least of her qualities."

"The Abbot's whore says enough," Giovanni Battista got to the point.

"How you refer to a lady," Alessandro was braver than he should be, "you've taken under your wing."

"Our sister is the lady." Domenico seemed to be assailing his brother. "Baccio speaks of an actress."

"Not only on stage."

Giovanni Battista's face reddened. "You're insolence isn't appreciated, Stradella."

"From what I hear, more than your *benevolenza*."

"What? Has she written to you? You can't have seen her. Not since she was with child. Why do I care for her?"

"Good question."

"I should throw her out."

"Signor," the page returned with a small bottle and cloth swab.

Alessandro grabbed at evasion. "*Cara mia,* sit down, *per favore,* sit."

"There's no need." Donatella didn't do as she was told without Alessandro forcing her backwards onto a stool as stylishly bowlegged as all the others—and most of the men—up and down that room.

He oiled the linen and dabbed her injury, blowing on it so his lips might touch her there, the heat coloring her cheeks.

The walk through a narcissistic hall was a distorted way to see herself—and not in her favor as she was turned to in disbelief and even disdain. But there was one opinion that mattered. Once they were seated Alessandro leaned over, warmly scented, fooling with her fingers and affections, offering another life, at least for an evening's attendance at an opera that wasn't his.

He seemed almost eager to escort her from one perilous situation to another. He must have known how she trembled, and not just in anticipation of the gods and goddesses about to sing and play. The moon was full in its setting, tense moments also waiting for something to begin as it had already, an overture playing on like a suitor for whatever attention he could get.

"*Vespasiano*. Why are they doing *Vespasiano*? It's idiotic."

There was murmuring as Alessandro uncrossed his legs and moved to the edge of his seat, waving madly. "*Vespasiano*. What could be done with it after it performed in *Venezia* without success?"

Heavy breathing and wide shoulders pushed in front of Donatella. "Signor, you're thinking of yourself."

"*Scuse, signorina*," Alessandro only apologized for his rudeness passing over Donatella with an attack on the unknown lady beside her, "And *signora*. Enjoy such shit, if you will."

"Shhh," sounded like the wings of angels, if ever they could be heard.

The opera was weak, but shorter than Donatella expected, for, as Alessandro didn't keep to himself, *grazie a Dio,* they left out the worst parts. Once his composure was gone he didn't mind who saw him bad tempered, sorry for himself, a bored child who wouldn't be entertained. He must come back to the purpose of more to do with music than society, and not merely for standing on stage again in a fancy coat with flared skirt, bowing over and over. He shouldn't try to live up to praise already received and holding him at ransom, but instead for immortality, like a painter on unsteady scaffolding, only for his art risking a fall.

"*Bène*, was I wrong?"

The woman beside Donatella directed a muted opinion to a companion.

Donatella wanted to stroke and shake him, relishing the genius but not quite regretting the rogue. "Only to make an issue of it."

"And would do so again."

She couldn't argue more. "Well, there weren't any sonnets."

His surprise was an expression of love. "You were there?"

"And you kept one," she felt pleasure in finally letting him know.

A roomful of strangers got up from their seats, some leaving immediately, others comparing exaggerated clothes and movements, puffed up hair and attitudes. The only ones acknowledging Donatella seemed to pity her.

"She doesn't miss you." Alessandro didn't need to point out Despina with two women and a man who had also offered Donatella their carriage and condescension.

"I'm glad." She put her head down.

"*Così,* I left a silly treasure unlocked?"

"No. Not silly."

"*Allora,*" his smile as telling as his words, "you're as sly as a fox—and I am."

"I didn't read it."

"Weren't you tempted?"

She felt flushed. "Yes, but I thought better of it."

"Ah." He looked around, the room almost empty. "I wonder."

"What?"

"That you're my least likely *nemesi.*"

"Certainly the least."

"Like Lonati. The *musica* is sweet, the reactions sharp."

"And so I'm single."

"No. Singular."

It was like being called courteous because she wasn't beautiful.

"With exceptional influence."

It wasn't any easier to be valued. "Nonna always said better to feel a compliment than hear it."

"Ah, I like that!"

He held her close to avoid unwanted attention, maneuvering out of the theater and into the palace's puzzle of halls that were wider than most streets in Genoa—and showier, as golden volutes, moldings, friezes, furniture, and greatly framed families were designed to make them. His impulse might have been hers—up a sparkling staircase and into the privacy of those who lived with spaciousness, opulence, and ancestry every day, except she wasn't as familiar with the privilege of antechamber, dressing, and sleeping rooms, not a fireplace lit, a silk fringed shawl borrowed for her shoulders. Double doors were a way out of trespassing and into the sky, the real moon breathing frostily and the city stumbling in rags and riches down to the bay where ships rose and fell darkly, the horizon flattening as the *Lanterna* looked on.

Across the mosaic terrace, the smell of pine was exhilarated by a frigid stillness contradicted by a half-embrace.

"Have you noticed how the moon dims the stars?"

"I rarely have a view of either."

"Except from my window." He remembered what she would never forget.

"You've been here before."

"I've been here before."

She hesitated, uncertain how to say what she wanted to, instead touching his face.

He was uncomfortable, especially with embarrassment, leading her off the terrace and back through the magnificent apartment. "I meant I'm no stranger to *palazzi*, if only for amusement. I first lived in one as a boy. It's how I got such airs and graces!"

She protested as he intended her to.

"*Sinceramente*, it was a time of study and expectations. Learning a trade like any fellow."

"Some things can't be learned."

"And I'm an example of that."

They hadn't quite left the boldness of a room containing a bed wider than it was long, headed by a three paneled mirror that returned admiration as much in gold as glass.

They heard voices, her name called in concern, his with suspicion.

"Maybe they'll give up." She really wanted to be lost with him.

"I can't let you miss your ride home. And we'd better not take this," Alessandro touched her shoulders more than was necessary for the shawl to fall before she did onto the blushing bed cover. She forgot there were only harbors for him while feeling at home in his arms.

"I'll go with you."

He just lifted her up. "It's not safe."

"Why do you say that?"

"Oh, no reason," he thought quickly, "except Golone attracts misfortune."

Despina was waiting for them to be found by a palace servant and found out by Golone.

"My wicked man." Alessandro played non-involvement well. "We haven't a carriage. And the night is cold."

"Unless we make it warmer."

"A long walk to *Luccoli*."

"Unless we rest on the way."

"Be careful," Donatella let everyone know how she felt.

"Well, we have a carriage." Despina snatched at her niece's arm. "Though, God knows, we're lucky. I've been instructed to put my foot down." She actually stamped; a young lady nearby laughed. "You act like a foolish and ill-bred girl. Hopefully not yet like Nubesta or any of that type, but what does it all look like now? Oh, you embarrass me so."

"You embarrass yourself," Donatella was less aware of what she said than of Alessandro on his way out.

Their cloaks were found while their transportation waited already filled with skirts, bosoms, silence, and one pair of heavy legs and cuffs, so that to fit in they had to become as small as possible. Who the other three women were hardly mattered, except her aunt thought they were important enough to be humiliated by. Donatella didn't need to wonder why the man, on the way there loath to speak, now demonstrated some privilege with a hand sinking into her lap.

Even when the carriage stopped he was attached to her bending out. She finally escaped him, but not the expectation that had come over her, as her feet touched the ground.

"I don't want to even suppose what went on. You've had too much freedom with him in this house. Now the whole city will know!"

Lidia had come into the hall to take their capes.

"Have you nothing to say?"

The girl barely looked up. "Would you like supper, mistress?"

"No. I'm filled with shame!"

"A glass of wine then?" the maid suggested, cleverer than her predecessor.

"What? No. All right."

Lidia's curtsey seemed a little crooked.

"Well," Despina waited for her to go, "Have you nothing to say?"

"I'm tired."

"So am I. Of everything explained or excused by art—or love. Finally I'm making strides in society, so I won't end my days destitute in purse or character."

"Just in your heart."

"I should slap you." Her aunt made no effort to do anything but continue complaining. "If you go to England I don't care what you do. Your mother and you can make tongues wag as much as you like. But in this city you will behave correctly, if I have to lock you in that ghostly room and throw away the key!"

Despina left her alone and Donatella loosened her dress and hair, taking off her shoes and tucking up her legs in the big chair by the window that, despite the cold night, she opened a little, her cats squeezing their noses to inhale what was off limits but not unimagined. She didn't need anyone else to lock her into the false security of giving up everything she had ever dreamed of to a personal *prammatica*, its ruling more subject to change than enforcement. Even with doors to keep her in and out, her life was as surprising as predictable.

She hadn't stopped waiting for another's footsteps, blessings and demons in mind, caring about Alessandro for joy and sorrow and selfishness. She looked forward to hearing his voice because of what it had to say to her, not others, except his music must involve as many as possible. She was his poorest and plainest patron, yet had all he needed to be remembered. If only there was more time and assets, and less to regret in the deep of the night disturbing but not stopping her from falling asleep before the tenant of truth and lies returned.

By morning she didn't know if he had or not.

CHAPTER TWENTY-TWO

So many bells on the hour, half, and even quarter hour. Day-to-day, the city and she were under siege from them. It was two months since she had written to her mother, the future near and far away, certain and uncertain, rumors suddenly silenced. And music, too, although Donatella hoped it was thought of, even if she wasn't.

Like the sea after a ship went down—as her father described it—everything in turmoil flattened as though what was gone had never been. Nonna had spoken of sinking, as well, into the cruelty of love. Too late for Donatella to steer away from a whirlpool of broad smiles and blue eyes, smooth hands and experience plotting a course through the fog her father thought he had cleared up. At the age of eighteen, Donatella didn't know if she had been saved for better or worse, who to thank or reproach, long for or wish never to see again. Fortunately or unfortunately, there was time to resist and accept that she wasn't meant for love's trick, settling somewhere between regret and freedom, never quite into extended maidenhood, attracted to the color in flowers instead of men's eyes, poetry on pages holding her attention and satisfying the need for a little stimulation.

There was something colder than winter, more smoke than heat in a house not well-situated after all, as narrow as tall, sheltered yet confined, private, and lonely. She had hardly slept while going through her grandmother's library, trying to decide what to take to England—if ever she went. Despina said she must if she wouldn't consider the options of staying in Genoa.

"You'll have to make up your mind, for I can't leave you in this house alone."

There were other things to be divided between her mother and aunt, like jewelry Despina considered immoral and yet knew the value of, dresses overtly theatrical except for lace and buttons and boning that could be decently re-used, underclothes and bedclothes too showy, even kept hidden. Nonna didn't have money; she had lived long past her ability to earn or need to spend any. She had just the letters and playbills and reviews that sustained her in the end. These were the valuables

Donatella meant to keep, along with the Venetian glass rosary Despina might yet think of but would never know what happened to.

Donatella put most of the volumes back on the shelves, tearful from the dust and distress that it was her aunt not grandmother she now listened to. Still, her real restriction was the certainty of what she would do if she didn't constantly consider what she shouldn't. So it wasn't just about missing those who took her fancy through their wild and wonderful impulses, as they were irresistible, indulgent, and exciting, remarkable for art and artfulness, destined for greatness and doomed as mere roguishness didn't explain, but also any chance to make something more daring of herself.

She opened the front door to footprints leading away through a dusting of snow, also noticing the hall floor needed cleaning. When she went to the kitchen for the mop, Lidia insisted she would take care of it.

Despina came in with her arms full of shirts.

Cook took them. "Doesn't Golone bring signor's laundry down anymore?"

"At least in that he knows better." Despina grinned with the victory of really running the house.

"The apartment must need attention."

"It's taken care of."

"Not by Lidia?"

"Only when master and servant are out, which is more often than not." Her aunt moved towards Donatella, her authority tinged with hopelessness at affecting her niece's hasty dressing. "You must wonder where they go."

"No."

"Good." Despina realized she might never be forgiven. "I'm glad."

"I'm not." Cook shook the flour off her hands.

"So you want her to be a fool or even worse."

"A foolish smile looks better than a frown for any reason."

"Well, Nubesta can't smile now," Despina thought she ended the conversation.

"Or is laughing at us all." Alessandro was on his way upstairs, Golone whining there wasn't any fun when he worked through the night. Despina murmured that the harpsichord and violin kept her awake.

Donatella was overly glad to have him there, and went in secret to her old room for the chance of hearing a little of his spirit composing itself. The creak of floor boards reflected pacing that eventually stopped, so she supposed he had either found inspiration or fallen asleep. She regretted that there was mostly the unknown in his disappearances, whether above or beyond her, vanishing into the clouds if not the sea, with all his worldly goods and a good deal of divine ones, too.

***

Anna Pamphilj's visit caused a commotion, Despina almost unwilling to receive her so that Cook headed for the front door, not displeased by Alessandro stopping her.

"You must find something to serve."

"Signor, my cooking is always fit for a king."

"Ah. But we need something as delicate as rich!"

Despina finally appeared. "What are you doing here?"

"What you wouldn't," Cook had become less and less deferential to her.

"But still the *principessa* waits." Alessandro let in the air of a cold afternoon and highborn lady, her ermine-edged cloak more defiant than pretentious. "You honor us."

"I surprise you." She held out a tightly gloved hand, but didn't let him kiss it. "Anyway, it is not me you need to impress."

Donatella didn't want to be there. Despina saw the princess' attention on her niece as something to divert. "Fortunately, there's a strong fire in the salon." Despina bowed quickly, uncomfortable with every part of herself.

"I hope I have not inconvenienced you."

"Oh, no. But if we'd known ...."

Princess Doria gestured to the shapeless servant who had stepped in enough for the door to be closed. "May she warm herself?"

"Of course."

"In the kitchen."

The princess took off cape and gloves, revealing a stunning burnished-brown gown pointed at the front, its umbrella skirt cut radically short over the yellow designs of another that was floor length and trailing. "It is February and still so cold, despite the city heating up with Carnival."

"We never go," Despina was stopped from elaborating.

"Why not? Such an opportunity to enjoy life. So rare in this city. You must join in this year."

"Perhaps," Despina didn't mean, directing the princess into the salon with irritable hospitality. "Nothing like you're used to."

"It is fine. I am sure Sandro thinks so."

"I keep myself to myself."

Donatella thought she misheard his answer.

The princess' was clearer, even through girlish laughter. "Then you are not the man you were!"

Donatella shut the door to her room but not before her cats ran out and Lidia was the messenger of a royal request. She took her time changing into a dress the color of the bay on an overcast day, trimmed with buttons like bird's eyes and braid that imitated myosotis flowers with some success. It fit better than for years, a sorrowful month having dropped some weight from her arms and waist. She sat at the dressing table, resurrecting what was appealing about her and dismissing what was not. Despina didn't say anything as Donatella hesitantly entered into sudden speechlessness and heat contrasting the chilly hall. Inviting scents and smiles couldn't have disagreed with Despina's scowl more, Alessandro rising and offering the seat still his when Donatella sat in it. On the settee, the princess had taken off her shoes to curl her legs under her skirt, small, dingy-stockinged feet peaking out.

"Please leave us," the princess told Despina.

Cook passed her, coming in with a plateful of little *focaccia* squares bubbling with garlic and oil, garnished with capers and parsley and filling the cluttered room, if not yet any mouths, with flavor. Alessandro poured himself another glass of wine, the princess only taking his smile as refreshment.

"He may have agreed," she informed Donatella.

Alessandro put his glass on the mantle and faced an unsatisfactory prospect with his back to the fire. "Do you need to be sure?"

"Sandro," the princess pleaded confidently, "I love you but you are exasperating!"

"The desired effect."

Donatella wished she understood more than being ignored.

"Look." The princess dropped her feet, her shimmering dress narrowing as she rose, slit sleeves like seedpods bursting, shoulders more exposed as they lifted. "I just want you to realize," she walked over to embrace his arm and stroke his hair, "that you must settle down."

"In *Genova*?"

"Wherever. No. In Genoa. You do have friends here."

"Ah." He relished the princess' touch, but his eyes looked to Donatella.

"Do not forget the old for the new." The princess couldn't have been jealous.

There wasn't a doubt Despina was listening at the door, as it opened at that moment and she attempted an opinion.

"We are not done here."

If Donatella revealed anything it was her unexpected affection for the great lady who waved her aunt away like a fly spoiling a meal, which reminded that Cook's effort shouldn't be wasted, either. She got up and with a fold of her skirt lifted the plate from in front of the fire, Alessandro reclaiming his original seat.

"Will you have her on your lap?" The princess' enjoyment of anything else was secondary.

Alessandro laughed, Donatella hiding her embarrassment by placing the plate back on the hearth.

"All right." The princess grew a little impatient. "Soon it will be the end of Carnival. You will come together or not. Do not let anyone interfere."

"Not even you?"

"Not even me." She lifted her glass to Alessandro's challenge. "Once I have left this house. Until then, sir, good fortune in fidelity."

His participation in the toast was more appeasement than agreement. Still the princess wouldn't give up asserting a plain woman could prove as compelling as a beautiful one, or at least that experience might be shown the benefits of inexperience.

"A fire can burn brighter and longer with the right piece of green wood than a crackly seasoned one," her musing was as impressive as her strong eyebrows, symmetrical curls, deep eyes, and attractively long nose. She pulled in her lips and skirt. "Please, there is room for you to sit with me."

Donatella accepted the honor and manipulation, not prepared for her face to be appreciated by a royal touch.

"I hope he has told you about your loveliness."

Both women, one more obvious than the other, looked for Alessandro's reaction.

"Well, at least he has noticed." The princess squeezed on her shoes and then Donatella's hand. "No, you two stay."

"Anna—" Alessandro also stood.

"Do as I say."

To Donatella's relief, he sat down.

"I must make amends with a less pleasant hostess." The princess' curls bounced in piles as her evenly laced back ended her visit, if not the awkwardness it had created.

"I'm sorry," Alessandro said first.

"For what?" Donatella didn't want to know.

"The weeks since we talked."

"Well, it's made Despina happy."

"And you?"

"Of course not."

"I see." He seemed about to leave it at that, getting up to move across the room to a sideboard, lifting the fringed runner from Nonna's spinet which he opened for a confident touch on its two octave keyboard.

"I would like to go to Carnival," Donatella looked down to the shape of her chest, "with you."

A strange chord threw his hand up. "Against orders?"

"Look who gave them. Look what gave them!"

"She's concerned."

"Or resentful."

"That you're not like her."

"I'm not."

The spinet's abandonment might have been hers, too. He walked around the room rubbing the darkness under his eyes. He stopped short of the door.

"It might be unwise."

"I don't care."

"No?" His mind was changed if not made up, coming to where the princess had left her. "I'm disappointed."

"What are we talking about?"

"Whether I'll take you to *Carnevale.*"

She was caught in a wishful trap, like the first time she had seen him. No, not really the first, for that was from afar and without any intent but to keep him in impossibility. It was when he blew in on scandal and forgiveness, delicate and dynamic, climbing to the top, carrying his fortune, mistaking identities but not character, his heart not skipping a beat so hers found some rhythm again. And from that beginning offered everything and nothing, working and playing, rising and falling, causing concern and relief, making music more important than memories.

"Do you have a disguise," he sat on the edge of the settee, his knees angling into her skirt, "or is this it?"

"What do you mean?" she spoke so softly she hardly knew what she said. "How do you need me to be different?"

"I don't." He seemed to apologize but wasn't sorry enough.

"Please. Tell me." She pushed her mouth onto his.

The most startling thing wasn't that Despina burst in or objected but how violently, tugging Donatella to the floor and pulling at her hair. Her aunt even kicked her as she tried to stand up. She didn't know it was Alessandro holding her until his voice, supportive, demanded, "This must stop!"

"Exactly." Despina was still slapping at Donatella.

"I mean, such *tirannia.*" He lifted an arm to obstruct a last blow.

"Does she know you sat on that couch kissing Signora Garibaldi?"

"You spy like a true *Genovese.*"

"You use women like a pimp."

"And you know what you speak of?"

"Please," Donatella cried, "I wish it would end. I wish Mama would write, and you would go to your ladies, Aunt. And you, signor, to yours.

So I couldn't stay here. Not in this house. Not in this city. Not in any way—"

"Now that's sense, my dear." Despina brushed herself down.

Alessandro stooped by the fire, shaking his head.

"It's not. Sense would be to fight for my life, not let the waves go flat."

"How clever you are." Despina grudgingly conceded as Donatella pushed her aside to leave both the argument and room. "It's a wonder you haven't compromised yourself before now, lost in poetry, and longing for sailors and artists."

CHAPTER TWENTY-THREE

Even the princess was misled. Her carriage returned the next morning with a delivery Alessandro was waiting for.

Golone emerged from the kitchen eating something. "So, Maestro, what will you be this year?"

"It isn't for me."

"Hey, I don't want to play the doctor again."

"I thought it *perfètto, Medico de la Peste.* You were almost suitably nosey."

"Very funny," Golone did appreciate.

"*Così*. This year *Pierrot*, the loyal servant."

Cook grabbed the cake out of Golone's mouth.

"I just meant to enjoy your delicious *panettone*."

"If only. With any luck you'll have your throat slit."

Lidia pulled on Cook's arm and crossed herself. Alessandro pleaded, too, with a different tactic: "My favorite cook, don't you forgive?" He lifted her hand to inhale its labors.

"For you, signor," Cook weakly pushed him away, "almost anything."

"Ah." Alessandro noticed Donatella with her back to a wall, beckoning her with the bulging package.

"What is it?"

He moved towards the stairs with a finger to his lips, Despina suddenly on the second floor landing as she might have been all along. "Are you well, *signorina*?"

"Of course. And you, signor?"

"It's time for *Carnevale*."

"As you know," Despina came down a step or two as he went up, "I think it's better to stay away."

"*Impossibile*."

Her niece passed her disapproval, too, Alessandro's encouragement relieving both women of their unhappy relationship.

"Don't worry," Golone said to Despina, "unlike me, he's the best of scoundrels."

Her reply was lost in Donatella's return to a dare and the third floor, another story for the stairway walls and ceiling promising to never tell unless she did.

Alessandro was laying her costume out on his bed.

"I can't wear that."

He looked her over as never before. "Shall we see?" He realized her concern. "The door closes."

She finally felt like a bride on her wedding night.

"Are you ready?" He laughed in the anticlimax of seeing she hadn't changed, and instead was holding up the dress like a shield. He fondled it around her shoulders until she grasped how it should be worn and he could reach out to the bed for the finishing touch. "*Carnevale* is about being there," the face of the disguise was surprisingly soft against hers, its ribbons tied at the back of her head, "as anyone but yourself."

"I see."

"For it's a well-designed *maschera.*" He paused, noticing as she did what was on the bottom of the table beside his bed. "Like a box trimmed with diamonds and gold."

"Oh, yes."

"One of a kind."

"I'm sure there are others." She tried to take back her enthusiasm.

A key turned, latch opened, top lifted. "Not with what's inside."

The box's satin lining mourned what impulse gave away.

An accolade for her?

"For safe keeping." He placed more than the present into her hands.

***

Sleep well tonight. She wished she had taken his advice, but she couldn't stop looking at the explicitly elegant gown hanging on the wardrobe. Nonna would have enjoyed the sight. It was silk and pearl buttoned, curving and billowing white, beribboned in sapphire and trimmed in bronze. Also warm and cold, tight and loose, depending on what the weather and outcome would be. A few hours later she was like a cat that had fallen from an open window, suddenly finding herself where she both longed and was afraid to be, feeling the hardness of pavement and softness of air.

Alessandro insisted she put on her mask again. "And practice on the way."

"Practice what?"

"Walking like a cat, purring like a cat."

"Really." She wasn't averse to doing so. "I've never seen a blue one."

"You'll see others turning green."

Although her face was immovable and pale, she couldn't hide her pleasure.

"All that's left is for you to rub against my legs."

Alessandro was all in white, as if he had absorbed winter from his hat like a boat with one wind-torn sail to frill topped hose and overly flapped boots. He was wimpled in lacy layers to his shoulders, tightly short coated and cavalier, out of fashion but not style, laddered rows of braid with buttons unfastened to the shine of his shirt also showing through gaping slashes on his sleeves. It would have been a perfect disguise but for the distinctiveness of his stride and attitude of his head exaggerated by a duckbill mask, the shine of his lower lip appearing when his expressive, unmistakable voice did.

Pierrot was at his own pace ahead. Alessandro never expected his servant to behave dutifully and wouldn't have enjoyed him as much if he had, making fun and opportunity of his negligence.

"It seems only Luccoli avoids the carnival." Donatella felt a little invincible herself, gone from domestication to prowling into the depths and shallowness of the city.

"Your aunt keeps it away."

The muddle of streets took them from crookedness to intriguc, banners of laundry to noble standards, crying babies to an absence of children, frying bread overpowered by roasting meat, and creativity in rags somehow competing with costumes of riches. Mayhem was soon spectacle, crookedness and free-for-all turning to conspiracy and costly antics, darkness into light, the sunny sky and *piazza* lifting and expanding the view towards the palace.

How Despina would envy her now. But no sooner than Donatella felt she had arrived, Alessandro was pulling her away.

"Put in your claws. The charade can wait; the *parata* will not."

He wasn't the only one who thought so. The rush was irresistible and crushing from behind and beside, bodies so hurried, with faces so still, voices muted except for the obscenities anonymity allowed. This was a *Genova* she had never seen, not even in stolen moments on and around her father's ship where profanity wasn't so public.

"Don't be shocked," Alessandro warned, holding her again with the same freshness that composed and conducted him into favor as well as caressed his way out of it. She saw nothing of the street or the church ringing its bells or any other building, as she was also both hidden and exposed in the riotous push to the city limits. Suddenly society was as mixed up as a stew, aromas fighting and mingling, its consistency thick and smooth, tastes hardy and delicate, altogether not too poor or too rich, bubbling with a shared excitement. Donatella was desperate not to be separated from Alessandro, for what way was there backwards or forwards without him? She needn't have worried, his voice distinctly above so much shouting or singing, in solo demanding *make way, make way for a questionable gentleman and his catty companion.*

"Only as she's soft and unimpressionable," he qualified when Donatella accepted his hand for all to see but not know who they were.

"Where are we going?"

"Through the gates of heaven." He appreciated her doubt. "Well, for now what's ahead."

"Look out!"

"They're coming!"

The warnings weren't about but for them, Alessandro too impulsive to listen to reason, taking her towards the city's east gate and not a moment too soon off to one side. They felt the sound and vibration of a near escape and then the way up a cold spiraling staircase that barely fit their feet or Donatella's skirt, Alessandro cursing that the second floor door to the battlement was locked. After pointlessly pounding on it, he went back down and out on the bridge, joining his lunacy to hers, hanging and waving over the parapet.

"*Bravo*! *Bravo*! All the city is a stage." He directed common chaos with more investment than a *cantata,* enjoying the artlessness in the strumming, plucking, piping and cranking, banging on pots, and singing from throats. He was even more excited by jugglers, acrobats, stilt-walkers, fire-eaters, monkeys, magicians, pickpockets, and pimps keeping a close eye on their harlots but also virgins with crowns and bouquets of flowers.

Nothing personified the spirit of *Carnevale* more than the *Commedia dell'Arte* characters of *Pulcinella, Zanni,* and *Arlechino* like puppets on strings.

"I should've brought my *violino*. Then we would be the cat and the fiddle."

She smiled because he assumed she knew that nursery rhyme.

"Hey, Maestro. I'm higher than you." Golone's voice was victorious at the top of the tower Alessandro had failed to conquer.

"Yet I have farther to fall."

They might have flown down to the street, trailing the parade less and less distinct from the crowd swollen like a woman with child who couldn't avoid shame whether legitimate or not. Suddenly Alessandro's handling of street songs in his confident tenor drew more attention and applause.

"Sing. As I know you can." he demanded of her.

She couldn't refuse him anything, not even the embarrassment of singing in the midst of more people than she had seen in her entire life. There was nothing familiar about the songs everyone else seemed to know, the dialect one she had rarely heard and barely understood.

"*Bravo* my *gattino*." Alessandro's carnival face leaned close to hers.

Before she could be pleased he gave into his proclivity for trying to seduce all the ladies open to him, which seemed to be the youngest and prettiest, although painted masks, high feathers, and low dresses might have made them more attractive than they were. It was amazing she didn't lose him there and then, the surge even more chaotic on its way back towards the ducal palace and into its square that embraced everyone and anyone on *Martedi Grasso.*

"We are here." A white glove signaled above heads and expectation. "*Per favore*. Make way. Make way."

Waves of revelers didn't know who directed them but calmed and parted nonetheless, so that Donatella found a fairly safe way through.

Still she nearly drowned in Alessandro's frothiness, belying his unfathomable depths, for he hardly wanted to take them to the restrictions at the palace's steps. Once there he tried to talk around the guards dressed as Spanish Captains, squirming as he searched in all those places a man's clothes might hold more than himself, finally displaying and kissing the paper with the necessary seal of approval. "We're in," he proclaimed, although they only climbed a few steps to the western entrance where nothing was rehearsed, overcrowded with inferior entertainment and other pretenders.

"We're not," Donatella murmured as they faced a large studded door, the merman *Triton* its knocker, two statuesque Dorias and an equally stone-faced guard standing alongside it.

Alessandro had his invitation ready.

"I can't let you in."

"There's no other way up?"

"That's the point, signor."

"Do you know who I am?"

"I don't need to know, signor."

"Come on, Sandro. There's plenty of wine and mischief down here." Lonati was coming up the steps.

"Ah. *Scaramuccia,* boastful coward. I'd know you anywhere."

No one could pretend to be hunchbacked with the straightforwardness of Lonati in silken black from head to toe, the *chittare* strapped around him suddenly swinging to his chest and nimble hands.

Donatella wasn't sure whether to be worried or amused.

"You didn't bring your violin?"

"No. I was invited to accompany this *signorina.*"

"I see." Lonati circled Donatella. "Meeeooow. Do I know this stray?" He lifted her cape and tried to lick her arm.

Alessandro slapped him away.

"Just keeping in character. A small, fast fray, little touch here, short attack there."

"How clever. Coming to *Carnevale* as yourself."

"The heavens have only one sun, but earth has many *Scaramuccias.*"

Alessandro was clearly frustrated, turning to the guard again. "Why not let us in?"

"I have orders."

"From whom?"

"Those who can give them."

"Please. It doesn't matter." Donatella touched his clenched hand.

Alessandro was as irritated by her appeal as by doors that wouldn't open. The bottle put in his hands was some consolation, like the music Lonati had already lowered himself to, surprisingly agile jumping around as he played the guitar and sang with a strong voice. Someone insisted Donatella drink and then dance, which she refused to do until she was spinning with anyone who was anyone else. She didn't know what she was doing or saying or hoping, her head lighter than her feet, laughing and crying, barely holding onto Nonna's opera cloak. And where was her dignity, passed from one to another, nothing as it seemed? Mockery and emulation were everywhere taking chances and changing circumstances so the butcher was a baker, banker a bandit, servant a master, noble a villain, man a woman, one attraction like another in the arms of a sailor.

The music slowed, a neckerchief recalling to her mind a time when she was not yet plain, a dance as intimate as it could be before it was interrupted.

The palace was suddenly open to Alessandro, and so to her.

"I have different orders now." The guard was still expressionless.

The early evening sunlight was very warm against their backs as they entered the palace, inside weakly illuminating a vast arching atrium from porticoed and fountained courtyards either side. Command as much as invitation hurried them across a marbled floor and up a double staircase, at the top a privileged and premeditated *Carnevale* custom-made in the finest fabricated layers, cock feathers and conceit sweeping and strutting and posing. The *loggias* were crowded with an entitled few increased by association. Shamelessness was bulging and dazzling, hedonism heightened and ambivalent in hair and shoes and sexuality, thin laughter and heavy scents. Music was a background to drinking and talking and dancing. There were even more daring activities in public rooms where heads lifted, shoulders turned, masks stared gorgeous and grotesque; a sense all the underhandedness of the city was there.

Alessandro didn't deny Donatella's concern but wouldn't let it stop them moving towards benevolent inspection.

The princess was waiting for what she had invented. Donatella curtsied and raised her sight to the golden features and rays of Anna Pamphilj, motioned closer by a chiffon sleeve and glaring ring. She tried to apologize, at least for stepping on the princess' skirt.

"My dear, my dear. You are here. That is what matters."

"You're generous, Excellency," Donatella also spoke gratefully for the clothes and chance given her.

"Is she not perfect?" the princess said to Alessandro.

He was spontaneous and deliberate, removing his hat and dropping his mask to kiss the princess' cheek, anything else he showed forever lost to the sudden awareness that they weren't alone with her plan. The prince offered the first and weakest challenge, giving his identity away by the skill with which his wife placated him.

It was more difficult to know who else protested, "Be careful of the company you keep, Anna," their interest moving from curious to morbid, murmurings soft and louder.

"Let the entertainer stay with the entertainment."

"To only play with their reputations!" A laugh didn't lighten the mood.

"But who is she?"

"A singer?"

"An actress?"

"She has the look of—"

"No one!"

"Sandro, take the almost English signorina away," the princess ordered. "Go find some merriness. There is none here!"

Alessandro drank a half-filled glass of wine from a tray, smiling until he masked himself again, swearing as he was stopped by a forceful arm.

"Signor Stradella, we don't mean to end your music making."

The mockery in white either laughed or shivered. "You couldn't do that, *Signore Lomellino*."

"And how do you know me?"

There was a pause. "As I do my own folly."

CHAPTER TWENTY-FOUR

The sun was going down. When they came out of the palace everyone was drunkenly good-humored and even deeper in deception, Alessandro wanting to catch up. An unknown minstrel offered him a *violino piccolo* but he let others show their talents and Donatella attention, which she discouraged by staying forbearingly close to him, even as he blew a kiss to a first story window. Golone was there and gone again, Lonati playing his part and the guitar comically. Donatella couldn't admit anything except being uncomfortable, not laughing at the joke or forgetting she might seem one herself. Instead she drank, too, faster than she could swallow, wine spilling out of the corners of her mouth.

"*Basta. Basta.*" Alessandro was hypocritical and correct in taking the bottle away from her. "Or you won't be standing for the fireworks."

She stayed alert if not steady, her body shrinking, stomach upset by not eating sooner and then too much grease and garlic, caught in an over-gathering of people as though her fate belonged to every one of them. She begged Alessandro to take her home yet was glad he refused. The stars formed constellations, shining and fading, rising and falling and looking down on them. There were oohs and aahs, hurrahs, and even applause for the elevated of Genoa struggling to be distinguished on the classically columned terrace, removing their masks so there wasn't any doubt who succeeded. "Are they performing for us, or are we for them?" someone asked and was silenced, torches held up with allegiance and even cheers. Alessandro pressed Donatella to consider another observation, turning them into lovers, hugging her back, his arm lifting. "Look there!" She didn't see anything but her undoing, actually closing her eyes and feeling what might do it, his body undisguised for a more private awareness of her own. There was an explosion and she jumped, settling into his humor and wondering if he could tell she smiled. "Ah, now you really are purring!" She couldn't stop what was happening, but who could? Over the bay a sacrificial piece of sky was torn apart, iridescent colors bursting and shooting and spraying, offering the spectacle of war without casualty, although there was no telling where its sparks landed and what might be damaged, as her father had learned when a fire on his ship smoldered for hours. "Enjoy! And damn the consequence!" Alessandro shook her, even lifted her, along with the crescendo of the spectacle. The known and unknown world illuminated, any clouds seeming to flee, doubts convinced captivity must take the chance of finally letting loose, *Genova* conceding there were no losers as *Carnevale* went up in smoke and out with a final bang.

Alessandro wasn't the only one carrying it on a little longer, at least until Lent was undeniable. But he made his own fireworks, ignited by drinking as much as quickly as he could and poking fun he thought he could get away with, finally taking Lonati's guitar and character, strumming like an amateur and bowing down to beggars and kings. *Scaramuccia* may or may not have minded but *Pierrot* certainly enjoyed master as servant serving a few *puttane* instead, touching their hair like the *Romano* and fondling their breasts, too, because there was no point in being accused of something he didn't do. Alessandro might have cared for a reaction other than the flattery of friends and curiosity of strangers, a street performer—albeit a superior one—courting an audience he didn't need for long, enjoying what he didn't understand, impersonating others to disown himself. He was in trouble and yet saw none in playing for a lower public and stakes, appreciating what appreciated him while not concerned with opinion. He wasn't alone in underestimating the risk; it seemed only Donatella realized its escalation in his stumbling and singing as fisherman or *basso*, then *castrato*. So he thought of what was higher than it should have been, going down to his hands and knees.

"Who are you? Gentleman or rogue?" someone in the crowd shouted.

"Is there any difference?" someone else joined in.

"Don't you know? Don't you see?" Alessandro crawled around, putting his nose to the ground. "Oink. Oink."

"No, who?"

"Are you blind? How can you not know?" He lifted his head and squealed.

"There are so many—"

"Enough pork for some."

"What a charade."

"*Mio Dio*! I'm Signore Lomellino."

"Which one?"

"You know. There's no mistaking. The *prosciutto crudo* of men. I go well with half-baked bread and onions. So I stink even more."

Alessandro got up and saluted the guards, ready to leave the *piazza* without their encouragement, insisting Golone do his duty if he could get his legs to move in any direction. They might have gone immediately home or even into the Cathedral for a glimpse of salvation, instead walking towards the port where the sky burning made the fog heavier and Donatella was always at risk of impulse. For once Golone kept close, for his own safety; unlikely he considered himself a chaperon. Alessandro didn't even hold her hand; he was quiet and almost sad as she followed him to the end of the pier to see what they could of the stars gone into memory, the new moon making the night old, the sea lost in the smallness of slapping against an aching dock. Although when the bells of the city struck midnight his voice was seductive—"Ah, so we remember what must be given up"—or so she heard it, convinced of his intention because of the embarrassment of her own. Of course there were still insecurities, Alessandro an alley cat to her fettered feline, knowing his way around the night and creatures offering pleasure and pain. There was no mistaking the remnants of flowers and fish and fowl in the *Piazza Banchi,* lending itself to commerce and corruption.

"Where *Genova* feeds and starves." Alessandro picked up the pace again with the excuse of needing to get Donatella back, "before Despina accuses me of abduction."

"Go on ahead and see if she's sleeping," he yelled at Golone.

"And if she's not?"

"In that case, this *signorina* must decide whether I'm to blame or thank."

Golone went grumbling on his mission, Alessandro detouring her down the Goldsmith's Way where, over time, vineyards had grown into a basilica. He removed his mask, loosened his coat, and looked up beyond the bell tower of *Santa Maria dell Vigne,* his eyes considering, chin confident, and advancement unstoppable.

"Where my *musica* will be heard next."

She might have asked if he had received a commission but was only interested in what he meant to her. They went back into the *Piazza*

Soziglia and crossed the *via Luccoli* where Golone, half-stripped of *Pierrot,* met them with a grin.

"All clear. Only the little nun awake, praying for your safe return."

"Her prayers are answered." Alessandro went through the gate and up to the door first, Donatella lagging behind. "You're thinking we should sneak in?"

"Not really." She tried to take off her mask, the ribbons caught in her hair, his cleverness untangling them and her second thoughts.

"*Così.* The housecat likes to roam after all." He held the door open, making sure her skirt swayed in before he did. His consideration wasn't all she needed. Golone was surprised to be on his own going upstairs as Alessandro followed Donatella to the doorway of Nonna's room where he whispered something she would never repeat and together they noticed Lidia looking curiously faithful as she was slowly shut out.

***

"Good afternoon."

"No one woke me."

"Not even your aunt? To accuse you of something?" He demoralized Donatella's already self-conscious entrance.

"She drinks too much herself."

"Which puts *colore* in the cheeks. But not the morning after." His remembering redeemed him. "What's that?

"A letter."

"My marching orders?" Alessandro readily sat back from his occupation, stretching his arms up, dropping them to shuffle the papers in front of him. "Or it's opened. So not for me."

"From my mother." Donatella was unable to look for long on his knowing her, trying to redefine her pleasure. "Oh, you're composing."

He took what she meant him too. "Ah, she writes in *Inglese.* And you can read it? How clever you are. And ready to leave me."

The back of the letter might have argued for her, but Donatella retrieved it before he might turn it over. *Today I did what I thought I could never do. I held your face in my hands and kissed your lips with my heart. And fell into the embrace of your arms as I already had with your soul.*

"When would you go?"

"Mama suggests April or May, so the crossing to Marseilles is fairly safe."

Donatella was prepared for his withdrawal, not the ownership of his arm around her, his hair blinding and smelling of ink.

"*Così*, you try blackmail. *Bène*, it won't work!"

"I wouldn't."

"No good ever comes of it." He held her tighter.

"But I wouldn't, ever."

And tighter. "Even heads broken!"

She struggled to breathe into his breast. "I wouldn't hurt you."

"How could you?" He was kinder in actions than words, remembering the responsive small of her back. "I must be getting old. Usually I'm as ready to run as some are to be rid of me. Which has made my life worse but my work better, another muse around the next corner, more beautiful, more dangerous, always unsettling. *Adèsso* here I am, as if nowhere left to go."

"You're just tired."

"I can't afford to be." He lay back on the couch, admitting some pain. "I hope I told you about your loveliness."

She wanted to hold the moment longer. "You have a headache?" She tried not to seem hopeful.

"No." He sat up so she could sit down, insisting she did, brushing the missive under his nose. "But if I did, for the cure of this *fragranza*. From a mother's hand? Or yours? Or both." He dropped it to his lap. "You mustn't delay your reply." He wrote on the air, "*Cara Mama*. I cannot decide ... between riding the waves of the sea," and then her breast, "or— as unpredictable— *Stradella*."

***

It wasn't a decision Donatella wanted to make, thinking about the orchids she had begun watering again, cultivating their waking from winter. Who would care for them, prop and protect them, turn and mist them, know when the light was too little or much and when to leave them alone? Despina was already gone although still there for appearances sake, managing some activities of the house and ignoring others, speaking to her niece if necessary and her lodger when there was no avoiding his existence. It helped that he was creating something respectable above her head, and that there weren't requests for more wine than a glass with dinner, or visitors except once when Lonati was briefly tolerated. Now and then Alessandro ventured out with folder and violin under his arm, a bored Golone at his side, and renewed hope that *Genova* continued to love him in spite of itself.

Donatella believed it would because there was no unloving him as he was, available and irresistible, artful yet authentic, larger than life but vulnerable. Making his acquaintance was unforgettable, seduction unavoidable, consequences bestowed like blessings. It was easier to believe he converted assassins than encouraged them and that he meant to fondle hearts, not break them. His wasn't a minor nobility, with the title *Il Maestro di Grande Spirito e lo Stile Fervente*, raising voices of angels from the aspirations of singers and offering chances for instrumentalists to perform miracles. So he gave an almost sacred consent to listening for salvation, revealing the purpose of a life not as undisciplined as it seemed. Every note was part of an arrangement between the gifts of God and man, with counterpoints carefully conducting discussions, harmonics cohering different expressions like a rainbow does its colors, language and instruments making passages into the same emotive poetry. Yet there was always innovation, interpretation, even impulsiveness and evasion, love never far from the theme, fulfillment not necessary to end with, drama as essential for content as the spectacle of a sunset burning up the sky when it never actually did.

It was only natural his mortality had opposition rising like the bow of a ship, the pride of its fleet greater against movement, stronger with something to prove, but reckless with perfection, risking his treasures on pirated waters. She couldn't see him satisfied with an easy voyage, let alone retired to any port, but might be his mooring whenever he was in her vicinity.

"Oh. You startled me."

He stood at the breakfast room end of the conservatory, dressed for going out. She was an artist, seeing him gracefully off balance like the orchid she was painting, bending left and then right, one arm behind a hip and the other lifting and falling at the same time, neck slightly turned, head back, and face flowering into a smile and wink.

***

Pounding on the front door was accompanied by Golone's yelling. Although it was locked after six or seven in the evening, without Alessandro he usually returned through the alley.

By the time Donatella stepped into the hall, Golone was there, a cape over his arm.

"Please, please, ladies." His concern was as strange as his entrance, although he couldn't hide his distress. "Go behind your doors. This isn't for you. Please!"

"What's going on?" Despina confronted him. "Keep your voice down. I suppose he'll come stumbling in, too."

"Please, signorina," someone spoke with authority and laid a hand on Golone's shoulder. "I also suggest you go where you won't witness more than is necessary."

Despina gasped and charged Donatella, wrestling her out of the way and yelling for Lidia to keep her there. But Lidia wanted to know, as well, hanging onto Donatella's arm, the hall becoming smaller than when a glimpse was promising and a harpsichord carried carefully upstairs.

***

Cook joined the stunned silence, wiping her hands on her skirt, Golone sidestepping towards the door he opened just in time for the stretcher coming back down.

"There's blood," Cook wailed and Despina understood what the movers were waiting for.

Still the functionary of public security lowered his voice. "Have you cleaned him?"

"And sewn him up."

"So quickly?"

"We know what we're doing."

Even the official was unprepared for their greedy frowns. "We'll need you again. Then you'll be paid." He pushed them out, grabbing Golone's sleeve so he wouldn't leave.

"No!" Donatella noticed her cats running to almost escape, too.

***

When she couldn't find them, she prayed they were just hiding, coming back into the hall to hear what her aunt didn't think she would.

"Did a doctor attend him?"

"Where it happened. And a priest, out of San Pietro, also not in time."

"Dear God."

"Too late, too late." The official was sympathetic. "Excuse me, signorina." Until he remembered Golone, investigation on his mind. "I need a word."

Golone squirmed, pulled into a corner where shadows and light hid some things and revealed others. "I saw nothing."

"You were walking with him."

"In front."

"To protect him?"

"Or leave him to himself."

"Rather insolent, for a servant."

"He didn't care about such things."

"He should have."

***

Despina's arms around her niece were surprising, not comforting, the voices of witness and inquisitor droning on, almost inaudible. *Piazza Banchi … why was he walking there? Returning home. Where had he been? Whom had he met? ... attacked from behind ... three times ... without a word ... fell flat on his face ... immediately ... no idea who did it ...*

"It's him," Cook accused Golone. "He's the murderer, like before!"

"Ridiculous. Who else would employ him?"

Golone was facing a wall, his arms shielding his breakdown so there was no denying what was over, the official saying something about needing to talk to him later, informing Despina that the body would be guarded.

"I can't believe it," she said.

"It's an ugly business, but not unexpected." The official looked at his notes that told him nothing more than when he had written them, his attention diverted from Golone walking up behind Donatella and pulling her hand back to put something in it.

***

She took an opportunity that wouldn't come again, climbing into darkness, thinking she mustn't be discovered except by one who would never reveal her secret. She felt her way, guided by memory and some explanation above. But the closer she got, the more inexplicable it seemed and should be, perfectly matched voices singing music she hadn't heard before and a soothing scent she recognized at once. She moved reverently towards disappearing, reaching the third floor and its paradisiacal ceiling, the door of discovery ajar so her intrusion was still welcomed. A candle served its purpose in the short hall, another in the long salon, and yet one more in the small bedroom where she found Alessandro in bed on his back as she had seen him sleep. There was bruising on his forehead and chin, his nose dislocated and bottom lip split, shirt unlaced, breeches knee-scuffed, and feet bare. *Where are his stockings and shoes?* The dampness of his hair and shirt could have meant he had washed before lying down, the stillness of his breathing that he had been drinking, the stain on his sleeve simply theatrics, like the blood-smeared parchment Golone had given her. She unfolded it, hardly grasping its message written in a lady's hand about an assignation that might have tricked its author, too. It didn't seem Alessandro was so hurt he wouldn't recover; no wonder he felt cold with the blanket beneath him and the brocade coverlet in a heap on the floor. *Where is his coat?* She made a still-life of arranging his arms like limp flowers in a vase, crossing his hands, her own becoming more desperate. *Where is his heart?* The house was silent, no one else considering him looking so lonely, his chances taken away.

She was the last to lay with him, covering him with her skirt and also smoothing his hair, wiping away her tears from his cheeks and her part in his story.

EPILOGUE

April, 1682. Two months and a day since something unheard of was buried in *Santa Maria delle Vigne*. Not the death noted by hundreds of candles and night long masses and a princess weeping in public less penitently than inferior ladies. Certainly not the tragedy mentioned in various *avvisi* and brought to justice and injustice for two thousand *scudi.* At least no expense was spared for the funeral, Anna Pamphilj insisting on its correctness with decent wrapping and a fine casket, bells rung and prayers said, music as celebrated as the man given a place in Genoa's most aristocratic churches and forgetful moods.

Despina had found Donatella with Alessandro before the police returned for further examination or the guard of honor arrived, even more upset when her niece seemed as lifeless as he did. Donatella slowly stirred without agreeing to live again; she concealed the parchment crumpled in her hand, Cook curious yet not questioning what she eventually threw into the kitchen fire.

Even without evidence and despite the long-established accusations of Alessandro touching too high while playing in the bass, it was reported he had such an accident because a mere actress preferred him. Just another of the *biglietti di calice* slipped to the *Minor Consiglio,* possibly by Golone panicking over who would employ him now. He was gone too soon to find out, not officially like Lonati and two other musicians asked to leave the city so they had a chance of being heard from again.

And what of the attackers, identities hardly doubted, seen shortly before and in the same place encouraging the greatest suspicion? Alhough the Lomellino brothers had more than one reason, there wasn't enough proof and they were released without any charge except a large fine. Beyond that, Donatella used her memories for holding on to love not hate, and a key even the landlord didn't know about when he locked up Alessandro's belongings until the time came for their listing and bequeathment. She wasn't a thief, something already hers in the copies she packed away with books and other things sent on to England weeks before her ship would sail. Despina left a few days after the funeral to be a lady's companion in a residence even further from the *Strata Nuovo,* taking the orchids with her. Signor Garibaldi let Donatella stay in the house as long as she needed, even helping with the paperwork required for traveling by sea and land. Cook decided to retire and live with a relative in *Casella,* a village in the hills to the northeast.

***

Long before it was light, Donatella woke to bells, trepidation, and anticipation, feeling sorry and not sorry, going backwards and forwards, forgotten by hope, accompanied by ghosts, and Lidia, who helped with hurrying, fixing her hair, finding all the laces and hooks of a new outfit, and praying over last misty looks into one room and then another. Donatella never meant to turn her back on a hero and his dragon, offering a bulging bag and then Lidia's smaller one to the carriage driver, the cats in a crate handled gently enough by those who loved them.

Crouched and pleading they might never get over being confined for so long; Donatella was not yet comfortable with letting them roam the cabin. Lidia lay limply on the hammock swaying even more than the ship, not heading out to sea as naturally as her mistress. For an hour or so through a small lookout, Genoa followed as if to always be there, stepping up to a precipitous high, offering its charm, boastfully admitting mistakes, surrounded by a world that didn't know whether to hold it or let it go, getting smaller but also more distinct haloed by the rising sun and yet shaped like a sliver of the moon.

Eventually there was only the wake of the journey to look at, a moving away in the water with such a gentle rhythm Donatella didn't believe it could ever be rough, inexperience not stopping her from being taken far from familiar shores. She pulled down the blind, fondled something in her lap.

"What's that?"

She didn't mind that Lidia saw what she carried, beautiful and courteous, rolled loosely, tied with taffeta and heartache.

ACCOLADE

How hath this city superb and sublime,
Reaching to Heaven in towers n' bells
Whilst the force of such paternal love swells,
So long avoided the heart's highest crime?
In appearance, for the sake of its rhyme
And reason, virtue of manners excels
Which nothing distracts and only foretells
Worship of one Savior at Christmastime.

***

Then steps up to this wise n' splendid stage
Maestro of Grand Spirit in Fervent Style,
Taking his bow after giving his best,
Raising notes, sights and hopes, for to beguile,
And apt by reputation to engage,
Breathing new life in her listening breast.

Genoa, 26 December, 1678

Alessandro Stradella (1639 – 1682)
Out of the Shadows

In 2002, while driving to work, I was fortunate to be near enough to the Canadian border to listen to CBC Radio 2, specifically a program called *In the Shadows*. The show highlighted the lives and works of artists—mainly musical—who for a variety of reasons had been largely ignored or forgotten. One morning a 17th Century Italian composer, whom I and obviously many others had never heard of, was featured. His music was stunning: fluid and melodic, with clear expressive vocals and distinct instrumentations. His story was replete with romance and intrigue, triumphs and tragedy, like an opera drawing on the divinity and failings of gods and men.

By the time I pulled into the parking lot at work, I knew why I was listening. I "knew" Alessandro Stradella. I recognized his distinct voice, his swaying form, his infectious smile, and his wandering heart. I had witnessed the rise and fall of his talents, how his music had showered him with forgiveness if not fortune. I spent the rest of that morning and many hours more in pursuit of him, my writer's urge "to do something with him" easier stirred than accomplished. He was so little on the pages of Google searches and music histories; a desire to create something significant out of my interest in him was soon frustrated and abandoned.

It wasn't until 2005 that I returned to Stradella as the novel subject I was looking for. The timing must have been right, for "suddenly" resources, although still not in abundance, were easier to find. As I read my costly used copy of *Alessandro Stradella, the Man and his Music* by musicologist Carolyn Gianturco, I found an opportunity for imagining my way into his story, focusing on his last fateful days in Genoa—not to change history but quietly humanize it, not merely to appreciate a great musician but personalize him, to reveal the ordinary in the extraordinary and the significance of the insignificant. Equipped with specifics and speculation, a growing CD library of his music, and a fictional female protagonist stepping out of my own hopes and disappointments, I was ready to begin.

The title and main setting of the novel reflect the strong possibility that Stradella last lived in a house owned by Giuseppe Maria Garibaldi just off the *via Luccoli* in Genoa, records indicating this was where his possessions were inventoried after his death. Born April 3, 1639 in Nepi near Rome of minor nobility, Stradella was cultivated but also something of a vagabond. His life seemed to be a struggle between the discipline of his work and the recklessness of his behavior. He had excellent opportunities, early on as a page for the Lante family, residing in their palace for many years; also to study music, probably in Bologna, and to advance a career composing and performing for the aristocracy, theater and church in Rome. Unfortunately, financial difficulties—or at least so he claimed—tempted him to participate in marriage brokering that upset a Cardinal who was also the Vatican Secretary of State, proving disastrous to Stradella's reputation in Rome, almost landing him in prison and "persuading" him to leave the city. From there he went to Venice, invited by one of his patrons, Polo Michiel, and soon employed as music teacher to Agnese Van Uffele, the "friend" of a nobleman who didn't appreciate Stradella's romantic involvement with her. Stradella ran off with Agnese to Turin where he hoped to find work. For a while he gained favor at court and apparently planned to marry her. Misfortune struck Stradella once more when two henchmen, probably sent by Agnese's Venetian nobleman, violently attacked him. He recovered, except for suffering bad headaches from time to time, but the marriage was called off and Agnese is never mentioned again in any of his surviving letters. Soon after, in December of 1677, Stradella accepted an invitation to the Carnival of Genoa. He decided to stay in the port city where he had friends in the prestigious Doria Pamphilj family and must have impressed other nobles, a group of them deciding to give him a house, food, servant, and substantial yearly stipend for no other requirement than that he remain in Genoa for a few years at least.

Throughout his career, Stradella's output was versatile and copious, including operas, oratorios, serenatas, madrigals, and incidental music. He worked royally and nobly for the theater and the church, for grand and domestic occasions, celebrating life and love, using allegory and heart and humor, challenging singers and instrumentalists and the inventiveness of himself. He developed the aria and concerto grosso, his work no less significant than Vivaldi's or Corelli's; if anything, more passionate and pioneering, his text interpretation and melodist abilities impressing Scarlatti and Handel, who freely borrowed from him.

Loving the wrong women and angering the wrong men held grave consequences and caused centuries of neglect for Stradella, who was a celebrity in his time. By the second decade of the 18th Century his compositions were rarely performed, the importance of his contribution to Baroque music eclipsed by the romantically enlarged legends that grew out of his life and death. He was the stuff misconceptions could so easily and profitably be made of, for the poet, the novelist, the so-called historian, and even other composers. Recently there has been some renewed interest in his music, but it remains obscure and underperformed as he only very slowly emerges from the shadows of his seemingly better behaved contemporaries.

Whether acting on a patron's whim or his own impulse, uncertainly and risk were inevitable for Stradella. It was his nature to embrace them, indulging in possibilities, captivating men and women known and unknown, seducing posterity with his reputation for making messes but also masterpieces. For a while, he enjoyed a fairly productive and settled time in Genoa. It wasn't to last. On February 25, 1682, about seven o'clock in the evening, in the *Piazza Banchi*, an unknown assassin stabbed him in the back, killing him instantly. His servant had been walking ahead of him and observed nothing until Stradella had fallen.

About the Author

I am a native of Buffalo, New York. My writing life began as a child retreating into the stories and poems that came to me, always believing that writing was the love I would keep and that would keep me. Early on I developed an interest in history, especially European history, while my participation in and appreciation of music was encouraged through memories shared about my maternal grandmother, who was a concert pianist in Chicago in the 1920's. My early pursuits also included drawing and painting—and acting, which I eventually gave up, admitting that my inclination for drama was better written than acted out, my imagination more consistent than my courage.

My educational journey took me from Theater Arts and Communication at SUNY Brockport, to a History and Literature major at Daemen College (formerly Rosary Hill College) in Amherst, NY; culminating in a dream-fulfilling semester at Wroxton College, England (run by Fairleigh Dickinson University, New Jersey), not far from Stratford Upon Avon, Warwick, Woodstock, Oxford, as well as the picturesque Cotswolds. Not least because of a fateful encounter, I impetuously stayed in Wroxton for sixteen years—a yellow-stoned village with thatched cottages, a duck pond, and twelfth century church and abbey turned Jacobean manor house. I lived, for better or worse, right off the pages of Fielding, the Brontes, Austin, Hardy, DH Lawrence, and even Dickens, surrounded by the beautiful hills, woods and fields of the Oxfordshire countryside, and all kinds of colorful characters. This truly turned out to be a life-changing experience that resonates in my personal and professional endeavors to this day.

I returned to the US in 1990, to a rural area of Western New York State where I still reside in a cozy log cabin with my beloved mother and cats. I have been employed in a variety of "day jobs" from retail to media consulting, as a volunteer coordinator for Western New York Public

Broadcasting, and presently with a career transitioning company in Williamsville, NY. In addition to writing, music, and art, I am passionate about nurturing nature and a consciousness for a more compassionate, inclusive, and peaceful world.

Please visit my website, where you can contact me: http://dmdenton-author-artist.com, and blog featuring my poetry and artwork: http://bardessdmdenton.wordpress.com/

ALL THINGS THAT MATTER PRESS ™

FOR MORE INFORMATION ON TITLES AVAILABLE FROM
ALL THINGS THAT MATTER PRESS, GO TO
http://allthingsthatmatterpress.com
or contact us at
allthingsthatmatterpress@gmail.com

www.ingramcontent.com/pod-product-compliance
Lightning Source LLC
LaVergne TN
LVHW020715110826
845149LV00012B/2281

* 9 7 8 0 9 8 5 7 7 8 9 7 2 *